GHOST IN THE MACHINE

KATIE O'SULLIVAN

Copyright © 2019 by Katie O'Sullivan

Second edition October 2020, Windmill Point Press

Cover art by Wicked Whale Publishing

ISBN: 978-1-7354061-0-7

Published in the United States of America

PROLOGUE

Saturday, October 12
Somewhere along Route 6, Cape Cod, Massachusetts

The speeding car slowed its pace a fraction allowing the back door to push open. She tumbled into the darkness, her body weightless as it flew through the pitch-black, down into the shallow ravine. Luckily, she landed on something that cushioned her fall. Not that it's ever lucky to be thrown from a moving vehicle in the middle of nowhere.

But still, she thought. *It's the little things.*

Surprisingly, she didn't feel any physical pain... Just dazed. Disoriented. She put a hand to her forehead, trying to remember why she'd been in the car in the first place. Nothing. No memory of why she'd been in the backseat or who drove the car that was now red tail lights fading in the distance.

The last thing she remembered clearly was leaving her

lawyer's office, phone to her ear talking with… someone. Arguing, but she couldn't remember about what. Another gap in her memory. She felt restless, as if she needed to be somewhere else right this minute, but at the same time she had no idea where that "else" might be. Or why she needed to hurry.

She put her hands down on the grass and attempted to stand but her body felt strange. Her legs didn't want to respond. "Not surprising, given the circumstances." Her voice sounded small and hollow, like it was afraid to echo into the surrounding darkness.

Cars and trucks whizzed along the two lane road several feet from where she was, headlights offering enough ambient light for her to make out the surroundings. Finally, she convinced her legs to try again and stood on the grassy bank to look around. Tall trees fenced in both sides of the road, with no billboards or storefronts or houses or signs of any kind to help her know where she was or even what state she was in. A line of those three foot yellow road dividers rose from the middle of the road to keep the traffic going each way separate from the other. Something about it seemed familiar, but she couldn't quite put a finger on why.

She looked down at the large black trash bag near her feet, the one that saved her from even more pain. A small rip in the thick plastic revealed a few fingers, their chipped nail polish nearly obscured by dried blood.

She covered her mouth, suppressing an involuntary scream as she backed away several steps. Her knees buckled and she sank to the ground, unable to tear her eyes from what she now knew was a body. A woman's body. Who was she? Why was she here by the side of the road like so much garbage? She lowered her head into her hands, the sadness devastating but no tears came. She'd witnessed so much tragedy in recent years that she couldn't say she was truly shocked to find an abandoned corpse by the side of the road.

But the idea of someone getting away with murder weighed on her.

When she looked up again, the rising sun brightened the sky and her outlook. She gazed up at the nearly cloudless expanse, vowing to seek justice for the dead woman lying so close to her. But first she needed to find help for herself. Funny that she didn't have her cell phone in her pocket; she never went anywhere without it. She rose slowly to her feet and thought about flagging down one of those cars zooming by. Would anyone stop?

An oversized white van pulled off the highway onto the grass, coasting to a stop several yards from where she stood. Yellowish lights flashed on its roof, giving it the semi-official look preferred by most highway departments. The side door slid open and several passengers jumped out into the grass, all wearing matching orange jumpsuits and reflective neon vests. The men carried trash bags and pointed sticks. A state trooper with a sharp-edged hat emerged from the front seat of the van and stood watching as the jump-suited men slowly shuffled through the grass.

"Barnstable County Correctional Facility," she read from the side of the van. Now the familiar-looking yellow dividers made more sense. She must be on Cape Cod, on the infamously narrow stretch of Route 6 known as "Suicide Alley." She'd been here before. Well, she'd driven down Route 6 in the past. She never sat on the grassy side of the road with a corpse before.

She raised her arm to wave down the trooper and his charges, but no one seemed to notice her. Perhaps the prisoners were instructed not to interact with motorists? One of the guys headed her way, walking straight toward the black trash bag. *He must see me,* she reasoned. He looked right at her. And then he focused on the trash bag at her feet.

Taking a few steps closer to the bag, she wondered how to explain why she was here by the side of the road with a dead body, something even she didn't understand. The sunlight reflected on gathered dew, the bag holding the body shining like a treasure. *Wait until he discovers what the treasure is,* she thought, grimacing. *And what happens to me? Will I be joining them in lockup?* She shuddered, thinking of the complicated circumstantial evidence. She'd been in court enough times to know situations like this were hard to explain away.

Wait, why am I familiar with lockup and courtrooms? Am I some kind of criminal? Something tickled her mind, but she couldn't quite grasp the thought. *Just tell the truth,* she told herself, taking a deep breath. *What's the worst that can happen?*

"Hey," she said as the skinny man in the orange jumpsuit approached. "I know this is strange, me being here without a car and all. Someone dumped me here, believe it or not. The same way they dumped her." She pointed to the bag.

He stopped short, his eyes riveted by the fingers poking from the hole. Thrusting his pointy stick deep into the grass, he turned away from the body. "Marvin! Bubba! Get the trooper. We got a problem." He turned back toward her. "Now who've we got here?" His beady eyes focused on the trash bag.

"I really don't know," she admitted, following his gaze. "It's a crime scene, though, so don't touch anything."

"I'd better not touch anything," he agreed, nodding his head along with his words. "Don't need no fingerprints of mine complicating things."

She looked up to see the trooper and several other convicts in bright orange running toward them. She sighed with a kind of relief, feeling as if some burden had been lifted. She'd been found. She could go home. Even if she didn't quite remember where home was.

"What've you got there?" The trooper's voice sounded deep and gravelly, as if he wasn't fully awake. "What's all this commotion about?"

"Officer, there's a dead woman in... " she started, but the convict spoke over her.

"Saw this bag by the side of the road. Saw them fingers poking out." He yanked his trash-collecting stick from the ground and used it to point at the tear in the bag. "I ain't touched nothing," he added.

"Everybody back to the van. Now." The trooper's deep, commanding voice brooked no arguments, and the crew turned as one to head back to the vehicle. He unclipped the radio from his belt. "Griff, I'm sending them all back to you."

"It hasn't even been ten minutes," complained his partner. "What's going on, Jack?"

"Looks like murder. Better call in the local cops for back-up." Jack returned the radio to his belt, and slowly circled the bag, still refusing to acknowledge the woman standing next to him.

"Excuse me?" she asked, confused that he was ignoring her. As far as he knew, she could be the murderer, or at least an eyewitness. "Don't you want to ask me anything?"

"What happened here?" His voice was low, not much more than a growl.

"I'm not really sure," she started, realizing that her lack of answers would definitely make her sound guilty. "One minute I was on my phone, and the next thing I know I'm being thrown out of a speeding car." She paused. "I remember bumping into someone on the sidewalk, and feeling like I was stung by a bee. Then, nothing until I woke up here."

The trooper didn't comment on her story. Instead, he kept looking at the bag and asked, "Who are you?"

That stopped her short. "I... I don't remember," she said, starting to panic. Why couldn't she remember her own name? She felt light-headed as she wracked her brain to answer what should be a simple question. The sun was much brighter now, higher in the sky. She looked up at it and felt a tremor run through her. "I need to sit down," she said and sank down into the rough-mown grass.

The radio crackled with static. "Jack?"

He unclipped the two-way and spoke. "Is back-up on the way, Griff?"

"E.T.A. seven minutes," Griff answered. "The crew's getting restless in the van."

"There's a dead woman here," Jack snapped. "Let them sit. Tell 'em it's better than picking up garbage."

"I think they're worried this might reflect on them somehow."

Jack grunted. "Reassure them. None of them are suspects."

As she listened to the troopers talk, she closed her eyes. When she opened them again, the area was swarming with uniformed men and women, both state troopers and local police officers. "I must have dozed off," she said out loud to no one in particular. No one seemed to be paying any attention to her, which she found curious. She was in the middle of a crime scene. How could they not notice her?

She stood and walked toward the man giving orders to the other troopers whom she recognized as the original guy on the scene. *Jack.* He was tall, with dark hair and piercing blue eyes, now that he'd taken off the mirrored shades. "Tell Griff to take those prisoners back. There won't be any more trash picking today. I'll get a ride with one of you guys."

She raised a hand to shade her eyes from the glare. "Excuse me, officer? I'm the one who found the body..." Her voice trailed off as she watched the body turn in her direction when they lifted it.

Her own face stared back at her, brown eyes open but sightless.

"It's me?" she whispered, unable to look away. "How can it be me? I'm not..." she looked back at Jack, still giving orders, and stepped directly in front of him, inches from his face. "Can't you see me? Am I really dead?" She reached out to touch his arm, but he turned his back to speak with someone else.

"No ID on her," one of the local cops said. "No purse or wallet in the bag either. Simmons thinks she was thrown from a car at high speed, but he says it's hard to tell since the prison gang got here first."

"The bag was torn," Jack reminded him. "I want the officers checking the area thoroughly in case her wallet or phone slipped out."

"Okay, MacDonald, we've got it from here." Two older men in dark suits stepped in front of Jack. "Let the real detectives take over."

"Pretty girl," one of them said, staring at her body. "What a waste. Another junkie on the trash heap of life."

She watched Jack's whole body go rigid. "Sir, I don't think she's your average drug overdose. If you look at the clothes she's wearing..."

"So she's a well-dressed junkie," the detective said with a smirk. "She's still dead, isn't she?"

"I'm dead?" she asked again, on the verge of tears. "That can't be right. Can someone please explain this to me?"

The law enforcement personnel swirled around her body, unable to comfort the ghost they couldn't see or hear.

1

Saturday, October 12
Barnstable County Medical Examiner and Coroner's office, Bourne,
Massachusetts

*J*ack MacDonald pulled his unmarked SUV into the
parking lot of the nondescript brick building. The
few other cars were scattered around the lot, most
likely fishermen taking advantage of an empty place to park on
a Sunday afternoon. Three other official vehicles sat close to
the double glass doors, letting him know the Medical Examiner
was open for business. He caught his reflection in the rearview
to adjust his uniform collar, his eyes the same pale, tired blue as
his shirt.

It had been a helluva long day. And unfortunately, it wasn't
over yet.

On the opposite side of the road, the Cape Cod Canal bustled with pleasure boats and fishermen all taking advantage of the long Columbus Day weekend to go after the striped bass supposedly running rampant through the local waters. He'd planned to do some fishing himself this weekend, until this case landed in his lap soon after dawn. His weekend shift was officially over, with PTO scheduled for Sunday and Monday of the holiday weekend, but he couldn't let this one go.

Jane Doe discovered in a trash bag by the side of the highway, no identification and no obvious cause of death. Probably drug related, judging by the track marks on her arms. But in his gut he knew something was different about this overdose, this woman. When he voiced his concerns, the detectives dismissed him with a laugh. State police didn't investigate homicides, they reminded him. Not even when they were the ones to discover the body.

Jack hoped the medical examiner could give him something to go on so he could at least track down the next of kin. He'd been the first officer on the scene and wanted to see this one through. Somewhere, there was a family wondering where this woman was. She was definitely someone's daughter. Maybe even someone's wife. Someone's mother.

No one deserves to be tossed aside like garbage.

In the passenger seat, Griffin clenched his cell phone to his ear, arguing with his ex. It didn't seem to Jack that his partner's divorce was going any smoother than his short but volatile marriage... but who was he to judge or offer advice? His last relationship hadn't gone any better, but at least Jack had the good sense not to marry her.

Not that he was against marriage as a concept. His dad and his three uncles had all been happily married for decades. It was a matter of finding the right individual, the one who felt like the missing piece to your personal puzzle. At least, that's how his cousin Ed talked about it when he married his high school sweetheart.

He thought he had that once, back when he was a college student and the world seemed big and shiny and filled with endless possibilities. Jack and Kristie had dated for three years, living together in Boston. After graduation, they both enrolled in law school determined to make a difference in the world. Then Jack's father ended up in a bad car accident and Jack took a leave of absence from school, rushing home to help with the recovery, and to help his mother run the family business. By the time he returned to Boston many months later, Kristie was dating someone new. Someone on track to graduate with her in June and move to New York City for a lucrative corporate job. She'd decided "making a difference" needed to include making a lot of money.

She told him he'd been selfish for abandoning their shared dream. For running home and leaving her alone in Boston for too long. She did her best to convince Jack it was his fault she'd fallen into bed with another man. While he knew what she said wasn't logical, he internalized the accusations.

He'd let her down.

Jack moved back to Cape Cod, bitter and alone. Instead of finishing his degree, he took the entrance exam and headed out to New Braintree in central Massachusetts, to the police academy.

A drunk driver caused his father's accident. A repeat offender. The lawyers and courts failed to keep the guy off the road, mostly because the cops who arrested him for DUI never followed up, never showed up in court, never saw things through. The guy was released back out on the streets time and time again. Until he almost killed Patrick MacDonald.

Despite what Kristie thought of him, Jack still wanted to make a difference. Getting out on the front lines seemed to be the fastest way. That was four years ago.

In the meantime, there were plenty of women to date during those long, hot Cape Cod summers, and he was in no rush to repeat past mistakes. No way in hell he wanted to end up like Griff, two years invested in a marriage doomed to fail from the start. A man should know what he's getting into before he says "I do." Otherwise, how can you say the words and mean them?

Jack always meant what he said. Always. *Despite the claims Kristie made to the contrary.*

Griff finally shoved the cell phone into his uniform pocket with a muttered curse.

Jack chuckled. "That good, huh?"

"Now she wants the dog. I mean, Baxter was mine before we got married."

Jack tried to refocus the conversation on work. "You ready for this?"

"Yeah." Griffin huffed out a long breath and stared out the windshield. "Is this how you imagined your life would be?"

"What're you talking about?"

"You know, when you joined the force. Did you imagine dead junkies and drunk drivers would be the highlights of our day? Supervising vans full of guys in orange?"

Jack turned to face his partner. "Is this about the job, or is this about Tricia?"

Griff laughed out loud and turned a wry grin toward Jack. "Tricia doesn't give two shits about me. Why would I waste my time worrying about her? More importantly, why're we still on the clock, spending our Saturday afternoon worrying about some junkie the local police dubbed *trash-bag girl*?"

"Fuck if know." Jack sighed. "It didn't feel like the cops were taking this one seriously. Everyone deserves justice. And that girl's family deserves to be notified sooner rather than later. You heard those detectives, they're going to look into it on Tuesday, after the holiday weekend. Like justice cares about taking a holiday."

"You take yourself and this job way too seriously, Jack. Which I assume is why you applied again to the FBI Academy. What? Don't look so surprised. You can't keep any secrets from your partner, you know."

Jack shifted in his seat, his uniform suddenly too tight around the collar. "Don't go talking about it. My family would freak if they thought I was moving away. Mom has this idea that since I'm pushing thirty I should be ready to settle down and start a family of my own, right here where she can babysit her grandkids."

Griff laughed again. "A family? Dude, you'd have to actually meet a girl and date her for more than a long weekend."

Jack responded with a middle-finger salute.

"You want my two cents worth of psycho-babble? You don't want to join the FBI, not really. You're a Cape Codder at heart. Maybe your mom's right. Find a girl and settle down. That'll take care of your restlessness."

"Yeah, it worked so well for you," Jack quipped, earning a punch in the shoulder.

"Enough of this bullshit stalling. Let's go see the Doc." Griffin opened the glove compartment, pulling out the pack of cigarettes they kept there for these visits to the morgue. He tucked one behind his ear before offering the pack. Jack shrugged and took one, sticking it between his lips but letting it dangle there, unlit.

"Dead junkies and drunk drivers," repeated Griff, shaking his head. "Maybe I should be the one trying to transfer."

"And where would you go? Your entire family lives on Cape Cod, just like mine." Jack frowned. "I'll ask you again, is it the job or Tricia you'd be running away from?" He reached over to grab his hat from the backseat, settling it on his head as he opened the driver's side door. "Let's go."

2

*C*old. She shivered as she glanced around the antiseptic white tiles of the windowless room. *How did I get here? What is this place? Am I in a hospital?*

A body lay on the stainless steel table, covered to the neck by a thin white sheet. Only the pale face and tangle of dark hair were visible.

She swallowed hard and tried to look at the corpse objectively. Dark locks disheveled but pulled away from the heart-shaped face. Clear skin, good bone structure, straight nose. Full lips surrounding a wide, generous mouth. The body underneath the sheet didn't seem too fat or too thin. She knew without a single doubt that this was her body... but who in the hell was she?

With a jolt, it came to her. "Cameron Nelson," she whispered to herself as she stared at her own pale face, lying lifeless on the table. She remembered her name.

It was a start.

Now if only she could remember what happened to land her on that stainless steel table.

How did she wind up *dead*? Was it an accident? If so, how did her body end up stuffed into a trash bag? The entire scene by the side of the highway seemed to rule out heart attack, aneurism, or any number of other "natural causes."

The door behind her opened, and an older man with grey hair and a white lab coat entered the room, a large black cat scooting in behind him before the door swung closed. The man passed through where she stood and Cameron shivered again at the intrusion. She wasn't used to being ignored, let alone having someone walk right through her body. It didn't hurt exactly, but it didn't feel normal. Nothing about the situation felt "normal."

The cat slunk along the wall, sticking to the shadows, staring in her direction as if he could see her. Could cats see ghosts? Cameron had no idea. She'd never had time for a pet, always busy, always on the go… doing what? That brought her up short again. In her mind she saw a fancy office and a desk covered in paperwork, but drew a blank on the rest. She stared back into the cat's luminous green eyes trying to focus on her own elusive thoughts, wondering how she could have forgotten something as basic as what she did for a living.

She turned to watch the man in the white lab coat. He stopped at the side table to don a pair of latex gloves. Why call a doctor if she was already dead? Why wear gloves to protect her if bacteria wasn't going to harm her? It dawned on her slowly that the gloves were for the doctor's protection, not hers, and this windowless room must be a morgue.

A place for the dead.

Which would make the doctor a coroner or medical examiner, one or the other. She knew there was a difference, but that didn't seem material at the moment. In either case, he was the one who would figure out how she ended up like she did on the side of the road.

The creases in the dark skin of his face and the coke-bottle-thick glasses told Cameron that he'd been at this job for a while. Hopefully he was good at what he did and would figure things out soon. Time was of the essence, of that she was certain, although Cameron wasn't exactly sure why that was the case. She was dead. It was too late to worry about saving her life. But she knew it was important that someone figure out what happened before... before...

The door banged open again.

A second man entered the room, dressed in a Massachusetts State Police uniform. Tall, dark haired and scowling, an unlit cigarette dangled from the corner of his mouth, large hands hanging by his sides. A jolt of recognition washed through her.

He was the state trooper from the side of the highway. *Jack*. Walking straight at her. Cameron quickly moved to the wall next to the black cat to avoid another trampling. Once was more than enough.

"Hey, Sam." The trooper stepped to the edge of the steel table, ignoring the sheet-covered body. "Haven't seen you in a while. How's Myrna these days?"

The dark-skinned man in the white coat, the one apparently named Sam, gave the trooper half a smile, his wrinkled mouth quirking up in a haphazard fashion. "Still nagging me to retire. Says she wants to move closer to the grandkids. I keep telling her Arizona is too far from the ocean. What would I do on my days off if I couldn't go fishing?"

The younger man laughed. "Sam, if you ever actually retire, then every day becomes a day off."

"Exactly. And there's still no ocean in Arizona." He shook his head and looked back down at the body. "Where's your partner, MacDonald?"

"Out in the lobby getting the details on the drunk drivers. Three bodies in a weekend seems like three too many. Teenagers, huh? A high school party gone wrong?"

"Something like that. Only I guess it went really wrong if they ended up here with me. Blood alcohol way too high. Wrapped themselves around an inconvenient tree. Griff couldn't talk with me to gather those details?"

Jack's lips twitched into an almost-smile. "Okay, you got me. He's hitting up your new secretary. Griff's divorce isn't going well and I think he's looking for a distraction." He chewed on the end of the cigarette between his lips, staring down at the body. "Do we know who she is yet?"

Sam shook his head and frowned. "You know you can't light that in here, MacDonald. County regulations. Plus my own personal prohibitions. I am a doctor, you know. Those things will kill you and I don't want to see you lying here on my table any time soon."

The younger man smiled for real, the grin lighting his entire face. Cameron realized the trooper was actually kind of cute, in a hard-edged sort of way. Close cropped dark brown hair, slightly ruffled where it grew longer at the top. Sharp cheekbones and a strong jawline sat above a thick, corded neck. The guy's deep voice commanded attention. And those eyes... not as piercing blue as they looked by the side of the highway, but intriguing nonetheless. Strong. Trustworthy. And right this moment looking a little sheepish to be called out about the cigarette.

"Actually, Dr. Miller, I don't even smoke. I read online how the taste of tobacco helps nullify certain odors. Gives me something to focus on, rather than the, uh, dead smells you've got going on here in the morgue." He looked down at the floor as he spoke, scuffing the toe of his black shoe along the tiles. Uncertainty laced his voice, which Cameron found endearing in such a big guy. As if he cared what other people thought.

Sam huffed out a dry laugh. "Lemme know how that works for you. I've only found one thing that helps with the odors around here."

"Oh yeah? What's that?"

"Whiskey. And lots of it."

Sam turned his back to the body and reached for the wheeled instrument cart, pushing it up next to the metal table and grabbing a clipboard. "Down to business. Initial toxicology screen indicates a drug overdose as cause of death, but we'll have to wait until tomorrow for the full lab report. The most interesting thing about the tox screen were the traces of sodium thiopental in the victim's blood, since that's not anyone's usual recreational drug of choice. But like I said, full lab report tomorrow will offer a more precise picture of the actual cause of death."

Jack held up a hand to interrupt. "You mean sodium *pentathol*? Like truth serum stuff from spy movies? The stuff they give James Bond to make him talk?"

With an exaggerated huff, the doctor looked up from the clipboard. "The proper nomenclature is sodium *thiopental*, and it's a rapid onset anesthetic barbiturate."

"In English?"

"It renders the victim unconscious with a fairly small dose. It still has widespread use in veterinary medicine but is considered a bit unstable for human use. We've found better alternatives over the years."

"How quickly are we talking? I mean with the unconsciousness thing, not the history lesson."

Sam glared over the rims of his glasses. "Less than a minute if injected properly. Do you want to hear the rest of the report or do you want a chemistry lesson too?"

"Just thought it might be important."

"And?"

Jack shrugged. "Proceed."

Another over-the-top huff. "Broken bones in legs and one arm are most definitely post-mortem due to complete lack of bruising. Most likely occurred when the body was thrown onto the side of the highway, most likely out of a moving vehicle, if the initial police speculation is correct, and I agree it seems to fall into place as a good working theory."

"I hear a lot of caveats in what you're telling me, Doc. Your reports are usually a lot more cut and dried."

Sam looked at him over his glasses for a second time, his face a blank mask and his voice devoid of emotion. "I've had the body less than twenty-four hours, MacDonald, and it's a holiday weekend. You're lucky I'm even here. Myrna wanted to take the grandkids to see the Grand Canyon for the long weekend."

"I've always wanted to see the Grand Canyon."

"Trust me. There's few things I want to do less than fight the goddamn traffic to Logan to travel by plane to Arizona, to then get in a rented minivan with three whining kids and drive for hours listening to cartoon soundtracks while they watch television in the backseat. Lucky for me, the oldest had a soccer tournament or some such nonsense, so I'm here instead."

Cameron watched the interchange with alternating amusement and despair. At this rate, her killer might never be caught. The thought triggered another memory. *Killers.* There had been two men, and they'd wanted something from her. *Information.* Maybe the trooper wasn't so far off with his truth serum idea.

The doctor was still scolding the younger man. "Now, if you're going to keep up with your own whining and complaining, like a preteen stuck on a three hour car trip to a National Monument you don't care to visit, I might have to rethink my priorities for the rest of this holiday weekend."

MacDonald scowled and took a deep breath, obviously reining in his own frustration. "Thank you for being here and for the preliminary report. But I have to ask another question. If there's no indication of foul play, how'd her body end up in a trash bag by the side of the road? Not too many junkies bag themselves up and throw their bodies away."

"Wait a minute! I'm no junkie!" Cameron practically vibrated with anger, startling the black cat at her side. "I've never done drugs in my life!" She might not remember much, but she was sure this was the truth. Another flash of memory. *Waking up tied to a chair while someone injected a needle into her inner arm. The cold rush of drugs entering her veins, the instant high. The onslaught of questions.* She had taken drugs, but not of her own free will.

If what the doctor said was correct, there was definitely "foul play" involved.

The men continued their discussion of the body – her body – oblivious to her ranting. "No identification or identifying marks. We'll run her fingerprints through the system, and if she's in there we should know her name by tomorrow. I can take dental x-rays and submit those to the database as well, but dental imaging takes a while to match up. Don't get your hopes too high for a quick hit, MacDonald."

"Why's that, Doc?"

"I don't think she's your run-of-the-mill junkie and I doubt she's been processed or fingerprinted. Women that look like this don't usually have prints in the system." He turned back to the body and nodded at her head. "Expensive haircut. Expensive nails. Hell, even the ripped clothing we removed had designer labels. Real ones too, not like the stuff Myrna gets at the discount outlets in Wareham. Maybe she's a washashore, but I'm guessing our gal is visiting Cape Cod for the holiday weekend."

MacDonald nodded. "I tried to tell the detectives something similar but they wouldn't listen to me. What are you thinking? New York? Philly? Boston?"

"Worcester," Cameron whispered, the one word coming to her suddenly as if bobbing to the surface of a deep lake. Although she didn't think that was quite right, it was the place that felt like home. Somewhere important to her. *Someone important lives there.* The cat stared back at her, nodding its head solemnly, as if she'd gotten the answer right.

"I'm thinking maybe Worcester," echoed the doctor.

Cameron's eyes popped wider when the words came out of the doctor's mouth, echoing her own. Could he really tell that from her body's clues, or could he hear her? How could that be, when no one else had been able? He'd given no indication up until this point either.

What. The. Hell?

The trooper chuckled. "Worcester, that's a good one. Does that even count as a city?"

"It's actually the second largest in Massachusetts, MacDonald. You'd think a trooper would know these things about your home state." The doctor lined up the instruments on the cart. "Are you staying while I cut her open?"

MacDonald shook his head, staring down at the exposed face above the sheet. "Let me know when you have something concrete, yeah? I'm sure she's got a family waiting for her to come home." Jack turned away from the table and spotted the black cat against the wall. "Hey there, Marley. What're you doing in the exam room?" He bent to scratch the animal behind its ear, addressing the other man over his shoulder. "Sam, you know you're not supposed to allow him in here during an autopsy. Could contaminate the bodies."

The old man's laugh sounded like sandpaper. "And you know it's not up to me what Marley does or doesn't do, Jack. He's been here as long as I have. You try telling him he's not allowed someplace. The damn cat thinks he owns the whole building."

Jack gave the cat one last pat on the head and straightened his legs. Standing this close, Cameron could tell he was at least six feet tall, if not a bit more. He radiated heat and strength and energy... and an underlying frustration. Was it for her? Her situation? Or something else entirely? He was different than most of the state cops she knew... wait, she was familiar with troopers? The jolt of awareness zipped through her, another clue to who she might have been.

Cameron watched Jack leave the white room, and turned back to see the medical examiner pulling the sheet down from the naked body lying on the cold steel. *Her* naked body. She felt no embarrassment, merely sadness at the lifeless shell left behind.

She agreed with the doctor's initial assessment as she saw no evidence of foul play, most of her skin perfect. No bullet wounds. No knife gashes. Some bruising on her arms. Nothing that looked serious. "What happened?"

"That's what I'm going to find out," Sam said under his breath, pausing to look up from the body. He faced her direction, but his eyes couldn't quite seem to find her. It was as if he was addressing the cat instead of her. "You might not want to watch this part. It might be difficult."

"Are you talking to the cat or to me?"

Another sandpaper laugh. "Marley doesn't care if I talk to him or not. He prefers the quiet. I think that's why he likes the morgue."

"You can... hear me?" Cameron asked, confused. He'd answered her question, but was looking in the wrong direction, still staring at the black cat. "Can you see me?"

He shook his head, eyelids shuttering as he sighed. "It's been my curse since childhood, hearing those who haven't moved on. But no, I don't see ghosts." He opened his eyes and looked down at the still, naked body before him. "I do see lots of dead people, though. Occupational hazard, you might say." He picked up a digital camera from among the tools on his table and began to snap pictures of the body, starting at the head and focusing on each part, each limb, individually.

"What're the photos for?" she asked, watching as he stopped to examine a spot on her upper arm and then move the camera in for a close-up. He moved on to the bruises on her inner arms. She took a step closer and was startled to see a series of small dark pinpricks inside her elbow. Needle marks. Several of them.

"I need to document the condition of the body," he said, pausing again as he looked at her fingertips. "Blue nail polish?"

"My sister visited and we got our nails done to match. She chose the color. It's called *Sea Ya Later, Sailor*. Wait... *Sister!* I have a sister! Whose name is..." another blank. A gaping black hole where a name should be. She gave a frustrated huff, annoyed by the missing puzzle pieces of her memory. "If I can remember something as insignificant as the name of the nail polish color, why can't I remember my sister's name? Or what happened to me?"

"You might not know what happened. Or you might not

want to remember." He put the camera back onto the instrument table and pointed to the place on the upper arm he'd been examining. "See there? The pinprick hole where the skin looks mottled, like you have a rash or an infection?"

She nodded, but quickly remembered he couldn't see her. "Yes," she said out loud.

"If I had to guess, I'd say someone injected you at that site a few days ago," he said. "A quick blood screen came back positive for opioids, which might seem obvious from all the track marks on your arms. But you also have sodium thiopental in your system, which…"

"I heard you explain that to the trooper."

The doctor nodded. "Okay. My point is this may have been the initial injection site, when you were given a strong, fast-acting anesthetic. The rest of the needle marks all seem fresh as well, injected over the course of a day or two instead of weeks or months, as if someone wanted to make you appear to be a junkie. What's the last thing that you remember?"

"I know I don't use drugs, unless you count vodka martinis. Besides, I'm afraid of needles." She thought back, pushing at the fog swirling in her head to retrieve the memories. "I was… hungry. I think I went out to grab something to eat, but then nothing. Black. And then I was being thrown from a speeding car, but I must have already been dead because my body was in a large bag and I wasn't."

"Do you remember who you are?"

"I remember my name – Cameron Nelson – and I think I might be from Worcester, like you told the detective. Something about Worcester seems important." She paused. "I guess I have a sister, if we got our nails done together. I remember being tied to a chair, and two men asking me questions. But I don't remember faces, or what they wanted from me. It's all so frustrating."

"Frustrating, but not unusual." He put the camera back onto the equipment table. "Especially in homicide cases. It'll come to you in time. It usually does."

Cameron didn't know how to respond. *Homicide cases.* She was no longer a person, just a case. *A homicide case.* It still didn't seem real.

She watched as he picked up the clipboard again and started filling out a form of some kind. She drifted over to the desk in the corner, where framed family photos mingled with piles of paperwork. The three grandchildren he'd spoken of earlier stood in a photo with him and a frumpy older woman with a huge smile on her face, Cinderella's castle rising in the background. Must have been a trip to Disneyworld. Normal. Ordinary.

She glanced back at the doctor and saw him holding a sharp looking scalpel. "If you're still here, you might want to look away." The blade touched down against the pale skin at the collarbone.

"I can't," she whispered, eyes riveted to the skin as the blade drew a straight line from shoulder to shoulder, and then down the very middle toward her belly. The blade veered to the left to avoid her navel and finally stopped at the pelvic bone. No blood oozed from the fresh cuts. "Where's the blood?"

"Your heart isn't pumping it anymore." He placed the scalpel back on the table and picked up an ominous looking saw. "You really should look away."

Cameron closed her eyes, feeling drained by the conversation. She felt the room slowly slip away, welcoming the blackness.

3

Sunday October 13, 12:03 a.m.
Green Street Apartments, Worcester, Massachusetts

*M*aggie Nelson cracked a sleepy eyelid and blew a strand of dark hair away from her mouth. She wasn't quite sure what woke her this early, especially considering she'd only crawled into bed a few hours before. Between working the late shift at the diner, studying for midterms, and fighting for studio time to work on her portfolio, Maggie couldn't remember the last good night of sleep she'd had, but it certainly wasn't recent.

Living in a low-rent student neighborhood of a college town didn't help her sleeping situation either, since someone was always out in the street making noise and an all-night party was the norm rather than the exception. Despite her sister's repeated offers to move her to a better apartment, Maggie couldn't take her money. Not when she really wasn't sure how much of it was legally earned and how much came from her sister's "side business," the one Maggie found out about when the cops knocked on the door of their shared Boston brownstone and arrested her sister.

Running a successful day spa in Boston was one thing. She knew Cameron's Newbury Street storefront, *Beacon Hill Beautiful*, catered to wealthy women and powerful men, offering everything from the usual facials and massages to the more exotic seaweed wraps and Dead Sea mud baths.

And also, apparently, sex.

The tabloid headlines from last spring flashed through Maggie's head.

SEX SCANDAL SHOCKS SOCIALITES

BEACON HILL BEAUTIFUL BOOTY-CALL

NEWBURY STREET MADAME ARRESTED

Getting tagged by the media as the *Beacon Hill Brothel* was a whole other can of worms. Stinky, slimy worms dragged through social media hell all spring and summer. Worms like her ex-boyfriend, a wannabe actor who'd sold his "inside story" to a Boston television station for a tidy sum. Despite being five years apart in age, the sisters looked enough alike that people often mistook them for twins, or mistook Maggie for actually being Cameron. Reporters hounded them equally, hunting for salacious details. Details Maggie didn't have because despite what was said on television, she didn't know anything.

Cameron didn't explain it to her either, except to apologize and say she'd gotten in over her head. Way over her head. Whatever that meant. You'd think shutting down the business and seizing Cameron's assets would be enough, but apparently not. Once the media got wind of the caliber of the clientele, a feeding frenzy ensued. Reporters wanted names. They wanted to "clean house" on Beacon Hill.

They wanted blood.

New headlines began to emerge in both the daily newspapers and the tabloids, alleging ties between the spa and the statehouse. The governor's name began to appear in the articles at an alarming speed.

STATEHOUSE SENATORS SOLICIT SEX
DID THE GOVERNOR GRAB SOME?

And the worst of them...

GOVERNOR PLUNKETT PAYS FOR PUSSY

Maggie dropped out of Boston's Mass Art and fled to Worcester at the beginning of the fall semester, enrolling at the New England School of Fine Art. She had one year left to earn her BFA, and decided to work full time at the diner to pay her own way. She also went from living with her sister in their serene Commonwealth Avenue brownstone to this cramped townhouse on the edge of campus with three other boisterous art students as roommates.

Thankfully, the trio were away on a road trip to UMass Amherst, also known affectionately as *Zoo Mass,* for the long weekend. Living with artists was never dull, that was for sure, with their mercurial temperaments and chaotic dating lives. Or maybe it was that Maggie was a few years older than the typical college senior. At twenty-five, she felt like she'd been there and done that, and wanted more than anything to graduate and move on with the next phase of her life.

Whatever that might be.

Wait! There it was again. The sound in the living room.

Did the girls return a day early from their road trip? She sat up in bed, wiping sleep from her eyes. She'd been looking forward to a whole Monday by herself, without having to waitress or deal with roommate drama. She needed to catch up on her portfolio work.

But if the girls were back early, something must have gone horribly wrong out in Amherst.

Another thud, this one louder, like furniture being overturned. That totally didn't sound like her roommates, no matter how crazy they might get on the weekends. Someone was definitely downstairs, and making a mess by the sounds of it. If it was Tasha and Crystal and Jasmine in the living room right now, there would be voices, laughter, and music accompanying that mess… something besides the eerie silence punctuated by bumps in the night. Those three never did anything without music. Or noise. Or laughter.

A shiver ran down Maggie's back. She reached for the light on her nightstand but it didn't turn on. Was the power out? A quick glance out the window confirmed the streetlights were still shining. So why wouldn't her lamp work?

She crept from her bed over toward the hallway, trying the

switches for her closet and the overhead light. Neither worked. It seemed the electricity to her townhouse was out.

Another thud downstairs accompanied by cursing, the voice rough and male.

Definitely not her roommates.

She tiptoed back to the bed and grabbed her cell phone from the nightstand, dialing 9-1-1 as she crouched down on the floor, making herself as small as possible. When the dispatcher answered, Maggie whispered her address into the receiver. "I think someone broke into my apartment. They're in my living room right now."

"Where are you, ma'am?"

"In my bedroom, upstairs."

"Does the door have a lock?"

"Umm, no?" Maggie swallowed hard, fully awake now. Her door wasn't even closed, let alone locked.

"We have a cruiser in your neighborhood. Stay on the line with me. Someone should be at your door shortly."

The pulse of her blood pounded hard and fast in her ears, drowning out any sounds coming from downstairs. "What should I do?"

"Stay where you are. Stay quiet and stay on the line," the dispatcher repeated.

"Okay," Maggie whispered. The swirl of red and blue police lights pierced her second floor window, dancing on the bedroom walls. "I think the police are here, but I don't hear any sirens."

"Officers are on the scene. Stay on the line," the dispatcher said again, her voice sounding almost mechanical.

Maggie felt like a coward hiding in her room, her heart beating a mile a minute. Shouldn't she do something to defend herself?

The pepper spray she usually carried was down in the kitchen, in her purse. Fat lot of good that did her now. She pushed the thought away. The police had arrived. They'd take care of things. "If I can see the police lights so can the bad guys," she said out loud.

A door slammed and Maggie bolted upright. "I think they got scared off. I'm gonna go down to check."

"Don't leave the bedroom, ma'am," the dispatcher warned. "Wait for the officer to announce himself."

"I'm just gonna take a peek," Maggie whispered, creeping toward the bedroom door and peering out. The hallway was pitch dark. Silence reigned. "I think they left."

"Ma'am? I advise against this," the dispatcher said, her voice louder in Maggie's ear. "Stay where you are."

Maggie ignored the warning. She lowered the phone to her side and stepped into the hallway. She flipped the light switch out of habit. Nothing happened. The phone still in her hand, she used the dim blue screen to illuminate the hallway and crept down the short flight of stairs, flipping the next switch as she went. Still nothing but darkness. "They did something to the power," she said into the phone. Before the dispatcher could say anything, Maggie switched on the flashlight app and checked out the living room.

Chaos greeted her. The couch sat stoically in its spot against the wall, but the pillows and cushions were strewn about the room as if thrown haphazardly. Every drawer had been torn from the communal desk in the corner, the contents dumped in messy piles on the throw rug. The floor to ceiling bookshelf was also knocked on its side and divested of contents, with books and knickknacks tossed everywhere. Broken glass from shattered picture frames caught the light and winked back at her like diamonds scattered amidst the rubble.

A sharp knock on the front door made her jump.

"Someone's here," she whispered into the phone.

"It's the officers on scene," explained the dispatcher. "They say they're at your door. You can let them in. I'll stay on the line until you confirm it's them."

"Gotcha. And thanks."

Walking the pair of uniformed officers through the apartment, Maggie pointed to the chaos. High powered flashlights lit everything in stark relief. One of the officers went back outside to determine what happened with the electricity. The other cop stood in the darkened kitchen, watching as she searched the cabinets for candles and matches.

"You live here alone, miss?"

"No, there are usually four of us but the others are all out of town for the weekend."

"You know this isn't the safest neighborhood to live alone, a pretty little thing like you. Lots of break-ins. People looking for stuff they can sell for drug money."

Maggie felt her face heat. She knew the neighborhood had a sketchy reputation with the local cops because of the nearby fraternities. "I told you, I have roommates."

He ignored her, scanning the apartment with disinterest. The majority of the first floor was an open plan encompassing the kitchen and living room with only the granite-topped island separating the rooms. A hallway led off to a bathroom and the two bedrooms that were on this floor, while the other two bedrooms and second bathroom were up the stairs.

"Can you identify anything that might be missing? Television? Laptop? Stereo? These junkies usually go for the portable stuff."

She shook her head. "There's no high end stuff. Is that why it looks like they were searching the place?" What could anyone possibly hope to find in a rundown student apartment? "We don't have a lot of electronics, since we're all working our way through college. Tuition is expensive enough."

"I know what you mean. I'm a recent graduate myself." He smiled before cocking his head to one side. "You know, you look awfully familiar."

A shiver ran down her back. "I waitress at Mike's Diner. Maybe you've seen me there?"

He shook his head. "Nah, familiar like I've seen you on TV or something. Are you sure you're just a student here?"

"Pretty damn sure," Maggie said, letting her agitation show.

The young cop side-eyed her and huffed. "Fine. No need to get your panties in a twist," he mumbled.

"Excuse me?"

"I said we should catalog your belongings to see if anything's amiss."

Totally not what he said, but Maggie ignored facts for the moment. After several moments of awkward silence, the second officer re-entered the apartment. He was slightly older than his partner, exuding more of an air of authority and less of the creeper vibe she got from the younger patrolman. "Electric wire leading into the house was cut clear through. I put calls in to the electric company and to dispatch. They're sending another cruiser to keep an eye on this block."

"Another cruiser? Why?"

The cops exchanged a long look she couldn't decipher. The older one spoke. "Cutting the power isn't the norm for this type of break-in. Seems more targeted as opposed to a random crime of opportunity."

She was baffled. "But why? The four of us are college students."

The younger cop cleared his throat. "Do you or any of your roommates come from wealthy families?"

She gave the creeper an incredulous look. "Are you kidding me? Would we live in this neighborhood if we did?"

"We're only trying to determine probable cause." The older cop turned back to his partner. "Have you secured the rest of the premises yet? Done a walk through or window check?"

She looked at the genuine concern on both of their faces and felt her pulse ratchet up several notches, her scalp prickling with anxiety. "I should phone my sister." The pair nodded and conferred briefly before walking away to check the rest of the townhouse interior.

Maggie found her phone where she'd left it on the counter and pulled up her contact list. She knew Cameron was preparing for grand jury testimony this week and wasn't sleeping much, so was likely still awake. Actually, it didn't matter if she were awake or not. Right this moment, Maggie needed her big sister.

"Cameron Nelson's phone," answered a deep male voice. Not her sister, but a familiar voice.

Maggie exhaled the breath she hadn't realized she was holding. "Hi Dan, it's Maggie."

She met Dan Koslov several weeks back when he'd joined Cameron's legal team, and they'd already spoken on the phone countless times. Dark-haired, well-groomed and totally easy on the eyes, he'd been the one assigned the position of unofficial bodyguard after the grand jury hearing date was set. It wasn't unusual for him to answer Cameron's phone. Maggie teased her sister relentlessly about the new "pretty boy" on her team, but Cameron insisted there was nothing going on except work.

Under normal circumstances, Maggie would take an opportunity like this to tease the shit out of both Dan and her sister. Answering her sister's phone at two in the morning? Come on. *How can they even pretend they were keeping it all business in the middle of the night?* But she'd save her teasing for later. Right now, she needed to hear her sister's voice. "I need to talk with Cameron. Right now."

"I wish I could help you but she left her phone with me again and went back to the hotel. I'm under strict instructions not to wake her for anything short of Armageddon." He chuckled as if he'd made an actual joke. "How's everything at work tonight? Gearing up for Halloween? Your sister told me the diner goes all out with the holiday decorations."

That was certainly true. Between the colony of bats hanging from the ceiling, the murder of fake crows gathered around the jukebox, and the oversized webs of black yarn adorning every window, not to mention the talking skeleton propped next to the cash register, Mike's Diner resembled some sort of cartoon version of a haunted house. But Halloween was the last thing on Maggie's mind at the moment.

She took a deep breath, tamping down on her frustration. "Dan, I really need to talk to her this time. It's important."

The guy chuckled. "Oh, you mean your call Friday wasn't important?"

She rolled her eyes. He'd been the one to answer her sister's phone a few nights before when she'd called to talk about plans for Thanksgiving break. "Dan, I'm serious. My roommates are out of town and our apartment got broken into while I was sleeping. The police are here with me now."

"Wait, what? Are you okay? Jeez, I thought Cameron said you worked Friday and Saturday nights at your all-night diner. I assumed...."

Maggie waved his words away before realizing he couldn't see the gesture. "No worries. And yeah, I work the late shift, not the overnight one. Two different things." She heard him swear under his breath.

"But you're okay? The police are there? Did they catch the guys?"

"I'm fine, just shaken. The police scared them off before they could steal anything, but the living room is a wreck. I'm having trouble figuring out if anything is actually missing."

"That sucks, kiddo." There was a pause. "Listen, testimony is scheduled to start in a few days and Cameron can't leave Boston... but I can drive out there. Help you figure stuff out. I'm sure your sister would be okay with that. She always says you're her priority."

"I appreciate that, Dan, but I'm fine. Really. I only wanted to hear her voice and tell her what happened. Have her call me as soon as she can, okay?"

"You got it. Hey, Cameron didn't give you any files to hold onto for her when you visited last week, did she?" He chuckled. "She's blaming me for misplacing shit, and it's totally frustrating. You know how she can get."

Maggie frowned and shook her head, before realizing yet again that he couldn't see her gestures. "She didn't give me anything. But I understand your frustration. I never want to get on her bad side either. You should ask Mrs. Johnson. Maybe she can help you find it." Anne Johnson was Cameron's lead attorney and a firecracker of a lawyer in the courtroom and on television. Maggie couldn't imagine anything escaping that woman's notice. She watched as one of the officers shone his light across the chaos scattered throughout the living room. "Right now it would be impossible to find anything in this mess. Tell Cameron if she can describe the files to me I'll take a look while I'm cleaning."

"Are you sure you don't need me to drive to Worcester?"

"Thanks, Dan. I'll be fine. You should get some sleep. And

hey, cleaning should be more fun than studying for midterms, right?"

"If you say so. Call if you need anything. Do you have my number?" He chuckled. "Not this number, obviously, since it's your sister's phone but my cell phone." He rattled it off, and Maggie grabbed a pen and piece of paper to jot it down.

"Thanks. Like I said, I'm fine." After a few more reassurances she ended the call, noting the orange lights now flashing outside the windows. She added Dan's number to her contact list as the two patrolmen returned to the living room. She touched the older guy's arm to get his attention. "Is it your back-up?"

"No, that's the electric company. They should have your electric in working order soon. Shed some light on the situation."

"Awesome."

He pointed his flashlight at his partner. "Carl, you stay here with Miss Nelson. I'm going to head outside to show them the cut in the line. Keep the door locked behind me."

After his partner left, Carl turned back toward Maggie. His flashlight trained downward, casting odd shadows around the room and across his face. She shuffled her bare feet along the wooden floor. "Did the rest of the apartment check out?"

"All clear." His eyes cut to the side before zeroing in on her again. "Your sister is named Cameron? Would that be Cameron Nelson, the Beacon Hill Madam?"

With reluctance, Maggie nodded her head, watching Carl's sneer return in full force.

"She's been all over the news for months. That's why you seemed familiar, you look exactly like her. All dark hair and pretty face and whatnot." His eyes slowly panned over her *whatnot*, his leer raising goosebumps up and down her arms.

Her face heated with embarrassment but her voice remained casual. "Yeah, I get that a lot."

"And I did see you on TV – in that Channel 25 tell-all your boyfriend did. You're famous too."

Anger crowded out the embarrassment. "Alex lied. And obviously, he's no longer my boyfriend."

"So… is this like the Worcester branch?" Shadows danced as he crossed his arms over his wide chest, the flashlight now pointed toward the chaos in the living room. The overturned bookshelf created eerie patterns on the walls behind the cop's bulky form.

A chill ran down her spine. "Excuse me?"

"You know. You said you and the other girls are *working your way* through college. How does a guy sign up for an appointment?"

"Uh…"

He took a step closer, invading her space, the dancing shadows making him seem bigger. Scarier. Menacing. "Maybe tonight's break-in had something to do with your business? An off-duty cop like me could provide bodyguard services. For a small fee, of course. I'm sure we could work something out."

What. The. Fuck?

A mix of anger and fear coursed through her, but she didn't step back even an inch. She stared up into his shadowed face, up close with the evil shine in Carl's eyes. If anything, that look made her stand straighter, fists clenched at her side. One thing she'd learned from her sister was to stand up for herself, and no one – not even a creepy cop – was going to intimidate her in her own home.

Before she could sort out a response, the lights came back on illuminating the hallway, kitchen, and living room in stark fluorescent light. She'd forgotten how she'd instinctively flicked every switch on her way through the apartment, but at the moment she was glad she did. The sudden change made Carl flinch backward, giving her some needed room to breathe.

The brightness chased away the shadows. Everything returned to proper proportions. Carl-the-cop didn't seem nearly as menacing with the lights on, his bulk now looking like the product of too many donuts rather than too many muscles. Not as intimidating now that she could see the weak chin covered in acne scars. He was nothing but a bully.

She hated bullies.

Angered by his insinuations and threats, she worked hard to keep her tone even. "Listen, Carl. I work at a diner. My three roommates work at the bookstore on campus. All we need from you is to find the guys who broke into our apartment. Got it?"

Carl huffed and seemed about to argue the point further before his partner called out to him. With one last leer, he walked away, leaving Maggie to survey the chaos around her.

4

Sunday, October 13
Barnstable County Medical Examiner and Coroner's office, Bourne

*S*am Miller inserted the key into the lock, pushing
open the office door. Columbus Day weekend might
be a holiday for most, but not for him. Not when there were
bodies to process. Cases like this one made him want to take his
wife's advice and retire now. "While we're still young enough to
enjoy it," Myrna kept telling him. Nagging, really.

Most days he ignored her. He smiled and nodded, drank his
coffee and came in to the office. He liked the quiet of the
morgue. Sam always knew how many spirits he could expect to
encounter here. No strange ghostly voices to pretend not to
hear.

There were a lot of voices around Cape Cod. So many

historic sites his wife dragged him to visit on his days off. Not to mention all the shops and restaurants in buildings that dated back hundreds of years.

So much history.

So many ghosts.

Maybe Myrna had a point. Not as much history in a place like Arizona, in one of those new suburbs near Phoenix, where their oldest child lived with his family. Where the grandkids lived. Seemed even more appealing on days like today.

The wall of stainless steel drawers was mostly empty, and utterly silent. Each drawer in this room of the morgue pulled opened like a filing cabinet, except instead of paperwork these drawers filed away lost souls waiting to find peace. At the moment, the wall held only the girl from the side of Route 6 and a pair of teenage boys from Falmouth. The boys took their pickup on a joyride after a few too many beers at a high school party Friday night, plowing into an oak tree. Their case was pretty straightforward. The families were notified from the scene. Their ghosts must have gone home with their parents, or moved on from this world altogether because Sam hadn't heard a peep from either of them.

Only souls with unfinished business tended to stick around the morgue.

Most bodies in Barnstable County were claimed right away. Of the fourteen counties in Massachusetts, Barnstable had the lowest unclaimed body rate. Not a lot of unidentified John or Jane Does when the medical examiner can simply ask the body what his name is and where he's from.

Sam enjoyed his job, although he didn't think "enjoyed" was quite the right word to use when it came to processing dead bodies. It was a profession where his particular ability, or disability as it were, came in handy to solve problems.

Granted, he didn't tell anyone about the extra-sensory way he solved some of the more interesting cases that crossed his desk. Not even his wife. Although, he was beginning to think some of the detectives he worked with suspected. Trooper MacDonald seemed to have his suspicions for sure.

There hadn't been an unsolved murder in his part of the state since he joined the office as a young doctor, just starting out. As the Chief County Medical Examiner, Sam Miller felt competent and needed, rather than awkward and out-of-place. At least in this job, he could use his gifts to make a difference. Even if it was only a small thing, like being able to notify the next of kin when a loved one was missing.

He pulled out the metal drawer and stared down at the lifeless young body lying on the hard cold steel. He'd uploaded her fingerprints and dental x-rays before going home the night before, along with the name the spirit gave him. He hoped for a positive match today, despite the holiday. Something about this young woman haunted him, and not in the usual sense.

Stuffed in a trash bag and left like garbage at the side of the road, as if someone was sending a message more than merely dumping a body.

But to whom? And why?

Lying there in the metal drawer, the girl looked young enough to still be in college. Her long eyelashes brushed almost down to her prominent cheekbones, like a sleeping pixie in an old fairy tale. Not like a dead druggie on a slab. But as he'd already told the ghost, she didn't seem like the typical overdose death. Whoever injected her full of opioids did a superficial job of making her look like an addict, although it was enough to fool the cops on the scene. Only MacDonald had bothered to follow up.

Why all the track marks? What did they do to her? He pushed the body drawer back into the wall, where it slid seamlessly into its place with an echoing click.

He turned on his computer to check email and get the day moving along. The cat jumped up onto the desk, startling him. "Damn cat," he muttered and grabbed his coffee mug so it wouldn't spill. He'd lost more than one keyboard to the nosy cat over the years. Marley strolled across the keyboard, the combination of keys opening a new screen with the young woman's records from the state database. A positive match for the fingerprints startled him, but it also meant he didn't have to reveal the true way he'd learned the woman's name. *Thank goodness for computers*, he thought as he read the information on the screen. *Makes everything much easier.*

"Did you figure out who I am? Or rather, who I was?"

He didn't bother to turn around because he knew there was nothing to see. It was the deceased; she must have returned to her body from wherever it was that spirits disappeared to from time to time. She sounded even younger than she looked on the table. *They all look younger in death.*

He tried to ignore her question. He couldn't see the ghost or feel her hovering presence, and it was almost easy to pretend she wasn't talking to him. After all these years, he was used to pretending. He'd learned at a young age that it wasn't considered normal to talk to people no one else could see. People questioned your sanity. His grandmother had been the only one who understood, as she'd been the one to explain the strange ability they shared.

Granny Miller left the South and moved to Cape Cod as a young woman to avoid the plethora of voices from Georgia's checkered past, the ghosts of slaves and lynching victims who still sought justice. She'd taken a position as a maid in a sea captain's household, one of the only jobs available to her as a sixteen year old black woman in 1890, one with no education and no family. She married a sailor and raised her family in New Bedford, making sure her children stayed in school so they would have more and better chances in life.

Soon after Sam was born, it became apparent something was different with him. Always talking to invisible people, long after the age when make believe friends were acceptable. It was Granny who took him aside to explain about the ghosts they could both hear whispering. "Think of it as a gift," she told him, "but one that you need to keep to yourself. People who don't have the gift won't understand. They can't. But you're a smart boy. Find a way to use it to your advantage."

While she didn't live to see him graduate from medical school, Sam figured she'd be mighty proud of the way he'd incorporated his gift, as she called it, into his career.

"Doctor Miller? I know you can hear me."

He sighed, returning to the present and reading the information on the computer screen. "Your fingerprints are on file in Boston, so yes, I have your information. Your name is Cameron Nelson, age 30. Your address is listed as Boston, not Worcester. Next of kin is listed as your sister, Margaret Nelson, age 25. Which does nothing to explain the drugs in your system."

"Margaret? That doesn't sound right. You would think I'd remember... Maggie. My sister's name is Maggie."

"Which is short for Margaret," Sam pointed out. "Does she live with your parents in Worcester perhaps?"

"Our parents died ten years ago. I've been Maggie's guardian ever since. She's still in college."

"There are several schools in and around Worcester, which

would explain your pull to the city. Let's see what else we can find out about you, and maybe why you've been arrested in the past."

"Arrested?"

"You've been fingerprinted. This mug shot is definitely your face. Let's see what else we can find out." He opened a new tab on the browser and typed in a search for Cameron's name. A list of several newspaper headlines filled the screen, and he clicked open the most recent Boston Globe article, dated the first of October.

SEX SCANDAL ROCKS BEACON HILL

The accompanying photo showed Cameron and another young woman standing at a microphone on the steps of Suffolk County Superior Courthouse in Boston.

"The Globe says you were involved with a political corruption case? Grand jury hearings are set to begin this month. Something about high priced call girls?"

"The little black book," the ghost whispered close to his ear, as if she were reading over his shoulder. Except that phrase wasn't anywhere on the screen.

"What are you talking about?" Sam waited, but there was no reply. He glanced around the cold, sterile room and wondered if the girl's ghost was still present. For once he wished his disability included *seeing* the spirits who insisted on talking with him.

The door to the hallway swung open. "Hey, Doc." Jack MacDonald strode into the room, out of uniform, wearing jeans and a flannel button-down, unlit cigarette once again dangling from the corner of his mouth. His eyes met Sam's and he stopped mid-step. "Something wrong?"

Sam shook his head. "Sometimes the job frustrates me, is all." He pointed to the cigarette hanging from his lower lip. "Still with the cigarettes? Those things will kill you."

"It's not lit, Doc. I told you before, I don't smoke." He stood next to him by the desk and gestured at the computer screen. "Is this our Jane Doe?"

"Cameron Nelson, age 30."

"The Beacon Hill Madam, huh?"

"You've heard of her?"

Jack shrugged. "I read the papers. How do the drugs fit into the picture?"

Sam huffed out a breath. "I'm not sure yet. Overdose was the definite cause of death, although she wasn't a habitual user or addict. If I had to guess, I'd label it homicide."

"Are you guessing or are you telling me?"

"I'm telling you." Sam pulled up the digital photos of the upper arm puncture wound as well as the track marks lining her inner arm. "She was injected in one of her triceps, with more sites in the usual places, but all the marks seem to be made within a day or two of each other. As if someone was trying to make it look like another victim of the opioid epidemic. Toxicology screen says in addition to the sodium thiopental there's also fentanyl in her system."

Jack grimaced. "One hundred times more potent than morphine, fifty times more potent than heroine. Not a drug to mess around with and easy to overdose."

"Whether the intent was to kill her or merely to incapacitate is unclear. It's a razor thin line between just enough and too much when it comes to fentanyl. Her death may not have been intentional but still homicide."

"Do we know her next of kin? Parents? Husband?"

"Unmarried. Sister at college in Worcester. Their parents are dead."

Jack huffed out a laugh. "You got all that from fingerprints and a tox screen?"

"And reading through the Boston Globe articles. Our victim is – or rather was – at the center of a political shit storm about to hit Beacon Hill." Sam rubbed a hand across his eyes. When he opened them again, the cat was seated on the keyboard. Another article opened on screen and Jack leaned over his shoulder to read out loud.

"*Beacon Hill Beautiful* owner Cameron Nelson claims to have information that could rock the state house and possibly derail the D.C.-aspirations of our own Republican Governor Charlie Plunkett. The Democrat-controlled State Senate is calling for closed grand jury hearings with possible impeachment proceedings to follow." He clamped a hand on Sam's shoulder. "Well, if that doesn't sound like a solid motive for murder, I'm not sure what else does."

Sam frowned and shook his head. "In this day and age, what kind of testimony could a brothel owner give that would hurt anyone's career? Especially a politician – look at the former President of the United States and his track record with women."

"True, but it would seem she knew something that was worth keeping quiet."

"My little black book," the ghost whispered close to Sam's ear.

Sam bit the inside of his cheek and waited for the ghost to continue, to chime in with more answers on her own. If he started talking to her in front of Jack, the proverbial cat would be out of the bag.

Nothing. Silence filled the room.

Jack cocked his head, his steely gaze narrowing. "Is she talking to you now?"

"What?" Startled, Sam tried for a confused expression, but he was afraid he only succeeded in looking guilty.

How did he guess?

Had he been that obvious? He thought he'd gotten adept at keeping this secret buried deep, but it was hard to talk with the living and the dead at the same time.

"Can this guy hear me too?" The ghost sounded excited. "I know he's a cop, but in my experience that means less than nothing. Most of them are part of the same machine. Is this one a good guy? Can we trust him? Can he keep my sister safe from them?"

"Who?" Sam asked her, before realizing Jack was scrutinizing every move he made.

"You know what I mean. I'm talking about the dead girl." Jack heaved a sigh. "Look, I know it's tough to be in a morgue day in and day out, and that you probably spend more time with the dead than with the living, but Doc, you need to keep your grip on reality. The poor girl is dead. She can't tell you who murdered her."

The cat stood and arched his back, walking across the keyboard once more, opening a new browser window. Both men turned to stare at the screen, showing a black and white image of Cameron standing with a shorter woman with large hair and a larger bust. On Cameron's other side stood two men conferring, heads down, backs to the camera. Both Jack and Sam leaned closer to read the caption. "Beacon Hill Madam Cameron Nelson with her lawyers and Monica Kazinski, Assistant District Attorney for Suffolk County," read Sam out loud before turning to face the detective, eager to deflect the conversation away from himself, away from any conversations he may or may not be having with the ghosts in his morgue. "Maybe this woman can give us some answers."

Jack's eyes were still glued to the screen, reading further. "This is breaking news from today. The A.D.A. was found dead in her downtown condo. Cameron Nelson is missing and the main suspect in the shooting."

5

Jack stared at the photograph on the doctor's computer screen. Two women dead. Did Nelson actually kill the A.D.A.? Or were they both victims of the same killer? And the big questions still remained – why?

The obvious answer: someone didn't want the grand jury testimony to go forward.

But killing a lawyer from the District Attorney's office? Presumably because she was privy to the details of Nelson's testimony. What about Nelson's own lawyers? Were they in danger now as well?

Sam stood up from his desk chair and began to pace along the edge of the room. "Does the article say anything about a little black book?"

Jack started to laugh at the cliché, but caught the serious look on the doctor's face. He sat in the desk chair to read the article more carefully. "Actually, it does mention something about a client list that Kazinski was set to enter into evidence this week. The reporter speculates the Beacon Hill Madam catered to many important figures throughout the Bay State, from the owner of the Patriots football team right up into the State House…" He lapsed into silence as he continued to scan the article.

No one knew whether an actual "little black book" existed or not. The media hinted it was the prime bargaining chip, but didn't say whether it was a literal physical book or a figurative list in the madam's head.

Either way, both the A.D.A. and Nelson were dead. There would be no bargaining. No plea deal for a lighter sentence. Someone already decided both women's fates – sentencing them to death.

Jack refocused his attention on the medical examiner. "Have you told anyone about her identity yet? Called the girl's lawyers or anything?"

"I barely opened the computer before you came barging in here this morning, Jack. Besides, who am I going to tell? You might have noticed the empty parking lot out front. Natalie will be here this afternoon because those teenagers are getting transferred to the funeral home later today. No one's going to be in their offices until Tuesday."

"Someone killed A.D.A. Kazinski in Boston and went to the trouble of driving a few hours to dump Nelson's body on Cape Cod. Probably hoping it would take longer to identify her this way. It was sheer luck we had the crew from the correctional facility out over the weekend and found her body so quickly. Having an extra day might be critical to solving both murders."

"Jack, I know you feel responsible because you were first on the scene, but this isn't your investigation."

Jack's excitement deflated. "You're right. Not my jurisdiction at all. *Fuck*."

"But… maybe you're right. I should try to reach someone in Boston as soon as possible. After all, if the cases are connected…" Sam paused, cocking his head to one side. Jack watched him closely, noting how his eyes widened.

"Doc is everything okay?"

Sam seemed to be debating with some inner voice of conscience. Jack waited, watching the other man's jaw clench tighter and tighter. Finally he blew out a long breath. "Okay, listen to me, Jack. I'm going to call the District Attorney's office, and let them know we have their main witness here in the morgue and that her testimony isn't going to be happening."

"Sounds good."

"But Jack, that poor girl is all alone now. She shouldn't be kept in the dark."

Jack frowned. "Who are you talking about? Both Cameron Nelson and the A.D.A. are already dead. Who are we keeping in the dark?"

"Cameron's sister, Maggie. I mean, Margaret Nelson. She needs help."

"You already said it yourself. Not my jurisdiction. My part in this mystery is over. I just needed to fit all the puzzle pieces together in my head."

"No, Jack. She needs you. You should drive to Worcester and let her know about her sister. I'm going to make the call to Boston, but you should go now. She should be the one to identify her sister's body, after all."

"Wait, what? That's like three plus hours driving with weekend traffic. Shouldn't you call her to come positively identify the body?"

The doctor gave him a disbelieving look. "I thought you wanted to be involved. It's still within your authority to notify the next of kin, and you're already over the damn bridge. It's only two hours at most to get to Worcester from here. Besides, the sister doesn't drive so you'll need to bring her here for the identification."

Jack narrowed his eyes at the older man. "What do you mean she doesn't drive? How would you know that?"

"No driver's license in the system," Sam replied quickly. "I already looked. I'm making an assumption that she doesn't drive."

"I thought you said you barely opened your computer? When did you have time to research all that?"

Sam ignored the question. "You need to do this, Jack."

"I'm not authorized to drive out there and bring her to Cape Cod." Jack wasn't sure why he argued the point. He was the one who found the body on the side of the road, and he was the one who was pushing to stay involved with this case. Yet, somehow he felt like Sam wasn't telling him the whole story. The doctor knew something he wasn't sharing, which made Jack uneasy. "Maybe we can call her?"

"No time for that." Sam seemed to be growing more agitated by the moment. "Look, I can tell by your lack of uniform that you're off-duty today, but I'm asking you, as a friend, to do this for me."

Jack narrowed his eyes and let sarcasm color his words. "Okay, you're right. I've got nothing better to do with my Sunday than sit in traffic. Oh wait, no. I'm meeting my cousins at noon to go fishing in Dylan's new boat. A drive to Worcester and back doesn't quite fit into the schedule."

"Don't be a selfish bastard. A girl's life might be in danger." Sam slammed a hand down onto the desk. The cat yowled and leaped off the desk, tearing off to hide in the shadows. "There are two dead women already. Are you really going fishing while a third girl is murdered?"

Jack held up both hands in a gesture of surrender. "Whoa, there, Doc. Don't you think you're overreacting?" He stood up from the desk chair and slowly backed away. "Is there anyone you want me to call to help you? Myrna, maybe?"

"You're not listening to me." He reclaimed the seat Jack vacated and pulled up another browser, typing quickly and then scribbling an address onto a memo pad. Tearing off the sheet, he shoved it into Jack's hand, pressing it tight. "It's barely nine o'clock now. You can be there before noon if you hurry."

Shit. Jack glanced at the paper now clutched between his fingers before meeting Sam's pleading eyes. "You're not going to let me say no, are you." It was more of a statement of fact than a question.

"I'm serious, Jack. A girl's life depends on you."

"So you said."

"You'll do it?"

Jack grimaced. "This is more than a little crazy. You know that, don't you?"

The doctor relaxed back into his chair. "You're a good man, MacDonald. Watch your back."

Shaking his head, he scrunched the piece of paper in his fist and turned toward the door. As it swung closed behind him, he could swear he heard Sam talking to someone in the room, telling them things would be okay. "Talking to that damn cat again," he muttered. "The guy's clearly losing it, and yet here I am doing what he says. Does that make me just as crazy as him?"

His instincts told him no. His neck prickled as he thought about the two women already dead and the looming political scandal they'd been involved with.

No, he wasn't crazy.

He pulled out his cell phone and dialed his cousin Dylan.

"I'm gonna have to cancel on you for fishing today. Looks like I'm driving to Worcester instead."

6

_____

Sunday, October 13, 10:37 a.m.
Green Street Apartments, Worcester

*A*s it turned out, cleaning up the mess left by the late-night intruders was *not* more fun than studying for midterms, despite what she'd told Dan on the phone. By the time she'd finished up with the cops, she'd been totally unable to get back to sleep. *Like seriously? After the crap that cop had the nerve to say out loud?* Maggie couldn't decide if it was worse when people judged her silently or when they came right out and said stupid shit.

Arrrgh.

Restoring the apartment to some semblance of normalcy was taking freaking forever. On top of the fact that the patrolmen stuck around for hours, photographing every last little thing as evidence. Because of course they took everything more seriously, after they realized who her sister was.

What an asshat. Once Officer Carl established that her sister was indeed the Beacon Hill Madam, his face took on a perma-leer and every one of his questions was either a double-entendre or borderline inappropriate. Even after she called him on it. How she paid her way through college was none of his fucking business, thank you very much.

She'd told him she worked at the local diner, in fact, she'd probably waited on him in the past. Lots of the Worcester cops stopped in for coffee and donuts at all times of the day and night. Countless night and countless cops all blending together. But Creepy Carl would definitely stand out from now on. And she'd most likely have to wait on him again in the future – him and his knowing leer.

Double arrrgh.

Having already straightened the larger items of furniture and moved everything to the side to vacuum up the broken glass, she found herself picking through the paperbacks, note-books and framed photos (sans glass) that once crammed the now-broken shelves. She sorted it into piles by owner so the other three girls could go through it all for themselves.

She texted Jasmine at 9:00 a.m. with a message to call home, knowing the women would never be awake until noon after a long weekend of fraternity-level partying. She figured when they awoke, they'd call and she could let them know the details before they walked into the mess that was their apartment. Tasha would probably pitch a fit, since she always got a little weird about anyone touching her stuff. Maggie surveyed the living room. Someone certainly "touched" her stuff. All their stuff.

A chill went down Maggie's spine, and she hugged her arms

around her middle. What if she didn't wake up last night? Would they have gone upstairs and found her? Another shiver ran through her. She felt so alone. So vulnerable. She needed her big sister.

Why hasn't Cameron called back yet?

Cold filled her veins. When she thought about her sister, a yawning emptiness surrounded her. Something was totally wrong in her world. She glanced around the room and amended that thought. *Something beyond the chaos in the living room. Something is wrong with Cameron.*

She'd always been what her family jokingly referred to as "sensitive." Not psychic or anything nearly as useful, but she picked up on other people's emotions, feeling them as if they were her own. If she cared about someone, she could tune in to their "wavelength."

At the moment, Cameron's wavelength was totally cold.

Thinking about it more closely, she realized she'd had the feeling something was wrong with her sister for a few days now. Maybe that's what prompted her call on Friday with the flimsy excuse of wanting to plan their Thanksgiving visit. Dan had reassured her then that Cameron was fine, that her sister was busy getting prepared to go before the Grand Jury.

God, if only Cameron would call. Cam would tease the crap out of her, like she always did. Tell her to get over the psychic mumbo jumbo and finish cleaning the mess staring her in the face. Cam was the practical sister who took charge and got things done. Maggie was the artist who couldn't make a decision to save her life, according to her family.

Maggie couldn't help what she felt – good, bad or indifferent. The emotional sensitivity, as she preferred to call it, tended to overwhelm her, but with time and therapy she'd learned to keep her feelings, and the paralyzing fear that accompanied some of those feelings, at arm's length. She was a functional adult now. *Yeah, right.*

The last time she'd felt this panicked – like she was a thousand feet underwater, the weight of it all crushing down on her – was the night her parents were killed ten years ago in a fiery pileup on the Massachusetts Turnpike. She was fifteen at the time and woke up screaming, having been visited in her dreams by the ghost of her crying mother. Maggie was alone in their Boston brownstone but called Cameron right away. Her big sister was five years older, and set to graduate early from Harvard Business School.

Cameron was less than sympathetic when Maggie first called, to the extent that she told her to grow a pair and get over her childish nightmares and fear of thunder. Then the state police knocked on Cameron's apartment door and informed her of the crash, their parents being two of the multiple fatalities on that stormy night.

In their absence, twenty-year-old Cameron became Maggie's guardian.

Over the last few years, her sister apologized for her reaction that night and took Maggie's intuition a little more seriously. Well, mostly serious.

The sisters might have had their differences growing up, but since the accident they'd grown close. To the point where Maggie could almost anticipate when Cam would call her. Or know when she'd show up on the doorstep unannounced. And the feeling Maggie had right now in her gut told her Cameron was in trouble.

Big trouble. But then again, Maggie already knew that. And had the guilty conscience to prove it.

Maybe the pressure of being named guardian of her younger sister sent Cameron over the edge of legality and sent her Beacon Street business into "bordello" territory to start with. Paying for college was not for the faint of heart, or the light of pocketbook. Was that when her sister turned into a pimp for the Beacon Hill elite?

Hard to say.

What Maggie did know was that her sister never let her want for anything, and found the money for the expensive psychotherapy and then found more money for college as Maggie struggled to find both a school and a major that suited her temperament. She finally settled on art. The art world thrives on emotional sensitivity and upheaval, both of which Maggie had in spades. She'd been in and out of college for years now, with graduation finally on the horizon for the coming spring. Then she could stop being a financial burden to her sister. Although… it was too late for Cameron to quietly stop the whole bordello business. Now that it'd been splashed across the news like blood at a crime scene, there was no going back to normal.

And now with this break-in, Maggie's sixth sense was lighting up like a Christmas tree, telling her something was wrong. *Shit,* she needed to get a grip on reality. Some drug-addled burglars broke into her apartment looking for quick stuff to sell to get their next fix, and suddenly she was worrying about her sister and their survival. And coming up with analogies dripping in blood.

Don't be crazy girl. Cut it out. She needed to get more sleep for sure.

The four piles in the living room looked like drunken anthills growing up from the wood floor. Of the four of them, Maggie had the most books in her pile. She decided to move all of her stuff to her bedroom. It would clear more floor space and make it easier for the others to maneuver once they got home from Amherst. Gathering an armful of assorted text books, notebooks and paperbacks, she trudged up the stairs and down the hall.

Dumping the first load against her bedroom wall, she glanced at her cell phone. Pushing eleven, and still no word from the girls. Clearly, none of them were concerned about midterms starting this week. Or texting her back. Could they still all be sleeping? Admittedly, she hadn't paid any attention to the weekend planning since she had to work Friday, Saturday and Sunday nights at the diner. There might have been plans for Monday brunch she didn't know about. Then again, her text to Jasmine had been pretty clear.

Our apartment was broken into last night. Call me when you get this.

She checked her phone again. Nope. No messages. No missed calls. Ringer volume turned up. Not only did her room-mates not return her call, but neither did Cameron. Maggie told Dan what happened, the break-in and the cops and all. He sounded concerned. He wouldn't have forgotten to pass the message along to Cameron, would he? Maggie knew the legal team wanted Cameron's full focus to be on the grand jury testimony, but this wasn't your run-of-the-mill distraction.

Her apartment was broken into. If they'd come upstairs and found her… if she hadn't woken up and called the police…. A shiver ran down the length of her spine as she pushed those thoughts from her head.

She woke up and called the police.

The bad guys ran away.

No harm done.

But… Maggie still needed her big sister.

Sharp knocking at the door echoed through the apartment. Heading down the short flight of stairs, she wondered briefly who'd be knocking. She wasn't expecting anyone and her roommates obviously had their own keys. *Maybe the police found the guys who broke in?*

A familiar face greeted her on the doorstep. *Speak of the devil.*

"Dan! I was just thinking about you. Why are you in Worcester?"

"Hey, Maggie." A wide smile split the lower half of his handsome face, mirrored glasses hiding his eyes. Despite it being the weekend, he wore a navy bespoke suit and starched white button-down. The absence of a tie was his only nod to weekend casualness. "They won't let your sister leave Boston until after the hearing, but she sent me to check up on you, make sure you're doing okay. Can I come in?"

She stepped back from the door and let him enter. He turned immediately toward the living room and the mess she'd been sorting through, taking in the broken shelving and the piles of books littering the floor. "They certainly did a number on the place. Have you figured out if anything is missing?"

"I won't know for sure until the others get home from Amherst. Can I get you anything? Water? Coffee? I was about to make a fresh pot." Maggie walked around the island into the kitchen area, grabbing the empty carafe and shoving it under the faucet. Caffeine and adrenaline were the only things keeping her going at this point, and the adrenaline was starting to wear thin.

"Coffee sounds good, but you don't have to wait on me. I came to see if you needed help, remember?" Dan removed his sunglasses and pulled one of the stools out from under the island. He sat facing Maggie, oozing Henry Cavill-levels of handsomeness all over her kitchen. "Tell me what happened."

Measuring the beans into the grinder, she recounted the story of being woken by noises after only an hour of sleep, and dialing 9-1-1 from her upstairs bedroom. She glossed over the part about Creepy Carl and his innuendos. While she would definitely be discussing that with her sister, it had no relevance to the current situation.

"The police are convinced it's junkies looking for stuff they can sell for drug money. There have been a lot of break-ins over the past year, they said. As far as I can tell, the burglars got frustrated that we didn't have a stereo or anything good to grab and decided to trash the place instead."

"Frustrated," Dan repeated, his eyes once again scanning the piles on the living room floor. "I'll bet they were frustrated. Look at all those binders and sketchpads and notebooks."

She frowned. "What do you mean?"

An indecipherable look passed over his face. "What you said before. Nothing good to sell for drug money."

"Oh, right." Beside her, the coffee maker gurgled and hissed, black gold pouring into the waiting carafe. "How do you take your coffee, Dan?"

"Light, two sugars," he replied in a flat tone, as if ordering at the diner counter.

Maggie tamped down on the odd feelings he dredged with his impersonal manner. No big deal. She offered to make coffee, right? She asked how he wanted it, right? He simply told her. So why did his impersonal tone make her uneasy? Or maybe it was the weird way he was watching her. Maybe because something was going wrong with Cameron's defense? *Oh crap.* Here she was, worried about picking up a little mess in the living room, while her sister's life was on the line. *Well, not literally her life. Her future for sure.* Even the infamous Hollywood Madam Heidi Fleiss was only sentenced to three years and released early for good behavior, but it's not like they'd give Cameron's business back to her when she got out of jail. She'd have to start over from scratch... doing something... and who would hire her after this media circus? Even a Harvard business degree only went so far.

She slid the mug across the counter to him. "How's Cameron's case going? I know you only joined the team at the start of September, but what do you think her chances are?"

Dan's brow furrowed. "Her chances? Maggie, you know she's guilty, right?"

She waved a hand to push away his words. "Yeah, yeah, I know that part. She made an error in judgement."

Dan wrapped both hands around the mug. "She pled guilty to the charges long before I joined the defense team."

"I know that. Believe me, I know. But the last time I was in Boston she said you guys were working out some sort of deal with the District Attorney's office? Isn't that what the grand jury hearings are all about?'

He sipped his coffee, staring at her over the rim of the mug. "Your sister always tells me to keep you out of this kind of conversation. Are you saying you know about the bargain she made and the evidence she plans to give?"

"Yes, of course. Well, sort of." She sighed and looked away, unable to meet his eyes. "Actually, no. I know she planned to testify but I'm in the dark about why. I assume it's got something to do with the rich guys who frequented the spa, and the fact they were paying for, um, you know..."

"Sex?" His tone was mocking. "C'mon, Maggie. You're twenty-something, not twelve. I'll bet you know all about the birds and the bees."

Maggie's cheeks burned, and she couldn't look at his handsome face and talk about sex at the same time. She took a deep breath, focusing on the broken bookshelf instead of his smirk. "When we got our nails done, Cameron said something about her 'little black book of vindication.' I assumed that meant names of people the District Attorney would be interested to hear."

"She told you about her notebook?" Dan's eyes narrowed to thin slits.

"She said the D.A.'s team wanted it for safe keeping. I assumed she gave it to them to go through before the hearings."

He barked out a laugh. "I don't think she would've given the only copy of her little black book to Monica's people."

She cocked her head. His laughter sounded a bit off. "No, I'm pretty sure she said she planned to hand it over. But she also said she wasn't sure who she could trust."

"Your sister's a very smart woman. Too smart for her own good, sometimes." Dan placed his mug on the counter and stood. "Enough chit chat. I drove all the way out here to help you."

She followed him the few steps into the living room area. Dan crouched next to one of the piles of binders and books. "Those belong to Crystal," she told him. "I tried to separate everything so the others could look through their stuff when they get back."

Dan glanced up at her. "Okay. Which pile is yours?"

She pointed to each pile in turn. "Crystal, Jasmine, Tasha, and mine. What I'd really like help with, though, is trying to figure out what to do with the bookshelves. Most of the wood is okay, except the one shelf that cracked, but I think all of the brackets might be broken. I suck at building – or rebuilding – furniture. Especially without the Ikea instruction book."

"Let me take a look." He dusted his hands together as he stood, removing his suit jacket and draping over one arm of the couch. After determining that yes, the crack in the one shelf was beyond repair, they worked together to get two of the three remaining shelves back into place. "I don't know, Maggie. That might be the best we can do without a trip to the hardware store. And another piece of wood to replace the broken one."

"I think…"

A knock on the door interrupted.

Maggie stared at the door. "Who could it be now?"

Dan shrugged and kept his focus on the shelves. "Your roommates?"

"They have their own keys," Maggie countered. "Maybe the police found the guys who broke in?"

"Wouldn't that be something," Dan muttered.

Maggie chuckled to herself. For a lawyer, Dan seemed to have as dim a view of the cops as she did, and she hadn't even told him the Creepy Carl story. Yet. Maybe she'd tell him later, and they could have a good laugh.

With a smile on her face for the first time in hours, she opened the door.

7

When the door swung open, Jack blinked hard before rubbing a hand over his eyes and blinking them again. The woman framed in the doorway was the mirror image of the body on the slab back in Bourne. The woman he'd found by the side of the road.

The one who was dead.

Tall and lean, dressed in worn jeans and a simple t-shirt, the woman with the rapidly fading smile was both hauntingly familiar and achingly beautiful. Long dark hair swept back in a messy ponytail, a smudge of dirt dusted along the jawline of her heart-shaped face while lively fire danced in her green eyes... it was as if the perfect porcelain doll of a woman laying on Dr. Miller's table came back to life.

He'd driven to Worcester to find and comfort a little sister, and yeah, he grumbled the entire course of the two hour drive. Berating himself for listening to Sam instead of heading to the fishing docks to meet his cousins. Two days off and he was spending the first one on a wild goose chase to placate an old man. He called Dylan to apologize for the last minute change in plan, but it's not like they could wait for him to get back on Cape. *Time and tide wait for no one.* Especially not for dumbasses who drive two hours to ease an old man's mind.

Jack didn't believe for a second that the sister was in danger, but it did seem like a helluva coincidence that both Cameron and the District Attorney were killed in the same weekend.

He knew the dead woman's sibling was a college student, but in his head he pictured someone younger. A kid who'd lost her parents, and now her big sister. Someone in braids or pigtails. He definitely hadn't pictured this heart-stopping beauty with the greenest eyes he'd ever seen, shining up at him like polished emeralds. And legs that went on for miles... legs he instantly pictured naked and wrapped tight around his waist as he pounded into her, hot and sweaty, driving them both over the edge into oblivion.

He watched as her smile faded, her mouth puckered into the cutest little bow of confusion, her plump lips looking oh-so-kissable, a slight indentation running down the middle of the full, perfect bottom lip. Something awoke inside him, a possessiveness that flared bright and took him by complete surprise.

Wait, did she ask him something?

With a start, he realized he'd been standing on her front steps staring at her gorgeous mouth, fantasizing about ravaging her body up against the door, his own mouth hanging open like a complete moron.

Fuck.

Apparently, it had been way too long since he'd gotten laid.

He cleared his throat, digging deep to find some semblance of professionalism. "Are you Margaret Nelson?"

Those emerald eyes narrowed. "I'm Maggie. Who the hell are you?"

Her surly attitude warmed him in a strange way and snapped him right back into reality. He straightened his shoulders and steeled his gaze. "State Trooper Jack MacDonald, ma'am. Can I come inside please?"

"State trooper my ass. Dressed like that? Show me some identification first, *Jack*." She held out one hand while the other gripped the edge of the door so tight her knuckles were white. She might sound tough, but she was scared. And she had a point. He'd forgotten he wasn't wearing his uniform, dressed in a flannel shirt and jeans for fishing with the boys and not for the official delivery of bad news. *The worst kind of news.*

He dug his wallet out of his back pocket. With his Smith & Wesson in the glove compartment, he was required to carry a badge even when he wasn't on duty. He grinned at her, hoping to melt a bit of the distrust from her eyes. "Totally understandable, ma'am." He flipped it open to show her his ID and shield, and when she hesitated he held it out for her to take. "Go on. I trust you."

Her fingers brushed his in the exchange and a shock zipped up to his elbow. Her eyes widened as she gasped. "Sorry! Some crazy static electricity, huh?" She went back to examining his badge. "Are you here with news about my break-in? I thought the local cops were handling the situation. Or did you escalate things because of my sister?"

"Maggie, your sister is... wait, what about a break-in? Someone broke into your house? When?"

"Last night. The police were here. Isn't that what you're here for, to update me on your progress?" Maggie crossed her arms over her chest, plumping them like soft pillows and drawing Jack's eyes inextricably downward. Pebbled nipples jutted against the thin cotton of her shirt as if in reaction to his hungry gaze.

"Eyes up here, trooper."

The heat of embarrassment washed through him as he met her amused stare. What the fuck was he thinking? He'd driven hours to give this woman the worst kind of news a trooper could deliver and here he stood ogling her tits like some wayward frat boy? He cleared his throat and willed his dick to calm the fuck down.

"I apologize for my rude behavior, ma'am. Can we step inside for this conversation?"

She seemed flustered for a moment, as if she'd forgotten they stood on the front steps. "Sure, come on in. I've got company and just made a pot of coffee if you want a cup." She held the door open wider and handed him his ID as he stepped over the threshold.

She closed the door behind him. "Dan's here helping me with..." She gestured to the room with books piled on the floor, a broken wooden shelf leaning against the couch. She frowned when she realized the room was empty. "Dan? I swear he was here a moment ago."

He watched as she walked through the living room and kitchen, as if her boyfriend were hiding behind a chair or the potted plant, then down the short hallway where three doors stood open and silent. He stood right inside the front door, shifting his weight, feeling a little deflated now that he knew there was a boyfriend in the picture. "That's okay, ma'am, I need to..."

"Quit ma'am-ing me, okay? I'm twenty-five, not a grand-mother." One side of her mouth tipped up in grin and Jack's stomach tightened into a knot. "Please call me Maggie."

"Okay, Maggie."

"Much better. Now let me find Dan." She headed up the staircase.

The sour flavor in his mouth tasting an awful lot like jealousy. It shouldn't matter to him that she had a boyfriend, in fact it would make this a heck of a lot easier if she had someone to comfort her when he gave her the bad news. So why did it feel like a direct punch to the gut every time the other man's name came out of her mouth? He just met her, for fuck's sake. She didn't belong to him.

He was here as a favor to Sam Miller. To notify the next of kin, nothing more.

No matter what his dick thought of the situation.

But the longer he stood there staring at the aftermath of the apparent robbery, the more uneasy he became with the situation. Something was going on that he didn't fully understand. Adding Maggie's break-in on top of her sister's apparent overdose and the murder of the Assistant District Attorney left Jack feeling like he'd stepped into a situation much bigger than the sum of the parts.

And Maggie was in the middle of it.

8

"There you are." Maggie stopped in the doorway to her bedroom. Dan looked totally out of place, sitting cross-legged on the floor and sorting through the pile of books she'd brought up earlier. "What are you doing in here?"

He glanced up at her, annoyance flashing across his face so quickly she decided she imagined it, his words calm. "I carried a stack of your books for you, and saw you'd already brought a bunch yourself. I was checking to see if Cameron's notebook got mixed up with your school things."

"Cameron's notebook?"

"Remember? Last night on the phone I mentioned we were missing one of her files?"

Maggie shook her head. "I thought you meant some sort of legal file. Something to do with the case."

"Trust me, this has to do with her case."

"Those are my sketchbooks and school notes, not legal files."

"I'm looking for her ledger with the names of her clientele. The D.A.'s office needs it for evidence." He turned away to focus on the notebooks again, opening and shutting each one as he shuffled through them.

She stared, even more confused. "I thought Cameron said she gave them the little black book already? Why would you think I'd have it?"

He remained focused on the books, restacking them from one pile into another. "She said she gave you a copy for safe-keeping."

"She… what?" Maggie had no recollection of Cameron giving her any book, let alone something as important as a ledger filled with evidence. A jolt ran through her, icy fingers of fear tracing down her spine. "Do you think that's what the burglars were looking for last night?"

He shrugged. "Maybe. Powerful people would prefer her book never sees the light of day."

"Okay." Her mind spun with scenarios as she watched him open and close each composition and spiral bound notebook as well as each of her various sketch pads, his careless fingers smudging the charcoals and pastels. He'd opened her book of landscape drawings and was staring at one of the renditions of a Boston skyline at twilight.

"Dan, if the District Attorney already has the original, why do you need the copy?"

He didn't look up as he flipped through the next few next drawings. "I think your sister realized she made a mistake. It's too dangerous for you to be involved, so she asked me to grab it and put it in the safe at our office."

"This would probably be useful information to tell the cops. Might be a lead they can use to figure out who broke into the apartment last night. There's a state trooper downstairs who…"

"What?" Dan's hands froze and his eyes darted to meet hers. "A state trooper?"

"Yeah, a Jack something or other, although he's not wearing a uniform." Maggie frowned, not understanding the sudden change in Dan's manner. Police were the good guys. Weren't they? As a lawyer he must work with cops all the time. "I made him show me his ID and he's got a badge. He's downstairs."

"You let him in?" Dan ran one hand through his hair leaving pastel smudges on his cheek and forehead. "Jesus, Maggie. You can't let strangers into your house, it's not safe. If he's not wearing a uniform how do you even know he's a real trooper? Those same guys from last night could be trying a different tactic and sent him to inquire about your sister's book. Has he said anything about Cameron?"

Another shiver of unease slid down her spine. What if Dan was on to something? The guy's ID could be fake, right? Jack seemed like a good guy, but who knew?

If anything, he seemed too sexy to be a cop. *Tall, dark and totally yummy. With eyes the color of the morning sky* – true blue, she called it when she tried to capture the sky with her pastels. The total opposite of Creepy Carl and so many of the other local cops who frequented the diner. She'd known Jack for all of five minutes, but she already knew he was the kind of guy who made her feel safe.

Her jaw clenched. No way was he one of the bad guys Dan referred to... even if the way he'd stared at her on the front steps made her want to do all sorts of bad things to him. With him. *Together, preferably in a very large bed.*

"Maggie?" The question in Dan's voice jolted her back to reality.

"Come downstairs. You can figure out if he's legit." She took a step forward and swiped at the pastel blotches along his cheekbone. "Oops, looks like you got some of my chalks on your face." Her rubbing spread the blue swath further down his cheek.

Dan caught his reflection in her mirror and grimaced. "Let me fix this first and I'll join you in a minute."

He went into the bathroom and closed the door. She allowed herself a smirk over his fastidious nature, but then hesitated at the top of the staircase, the sliver of doubt returning. What if Dan was right and Jack wasn't really a cop? She'd had those uneasy feelings all morning, like something bad was about to happen. What if Jack's arrival was part of it?

Taking a deep breath, she squared her shoulders and headed down the stairs. Whether Jack was part of it or not, her gut said to trust him.

She found him coming back in through the now open front door. His flannel shirt was untucked at the waist, and somehow the more casual look made him seem even hotter, like some kind of sexy cowboy. All he needed was a Stetson and he could lasso her right into his arms. She rolled her eyes at her own thoughts. *Too many romance novels.*

He jerked a thumb to the front door, those true blue eyes wary as if sensing her apprehension. "I forgot something in the car. Everything okay with your boyfriend?"

"Dan's not my boyfriend," she replied a little too quickly. She swallowed and willed herself to take it slow. Just because she thought he was sex-on-a-stick didn't mean she was going to throw herself at him. Or that he was going to throw himself at her. *Take a deep breath, Maggie.* "He's a lawyer. Dan Koslov. On my sister's legal team. Cameron sent him here to check on me after the break-in last night."

"She... sent him? Tell me what that means." Jack's eyes narrowed to slits and his hard chin jutted forward, making him look a bit dangerous. She could practically hear his teeth clenching. Had she totally misread the situation? Was Dan correct and this guy wasn't exactly who he said he was?

She crossed her arms over her chest again, feeling uneasy. She hoped Dan hurried up in the bathroom. "Well, you know who my sister is, right? Cameron Nelson?"

He nodded and gestured for her to continue. She could see the muscles along his jaw tensing even more.

"She's prepping with her legal team to testify later this week. Dan said they won't let her leave Boston right now and sent him to check on me instead."

"Maggie, he's lying. Your sister wasn't in Boston last night. She's not in Boston today either."

She frowned. "What are you talking about? Of course she's there. Getting ready to testify. Dan told me."

"And where is this Dan person right now?" He took several steps toward her as he spoke.

"Upstairs in the bathroom. Why?"

"I need to tell you something. It's your sister Cameron. She…"

A metallic click echoed in the room. "Stop right there. Don't say another word." Turning toward his voice, she saw Dan halfway down the stairs, aiming a handgun at Jack. "Back away from the girl."

Alarmed, she stepped in front of Jack, arms out wide blocking Dan's intended target. She might not know Jack's motives or understand why he thought Dan was lying, but she certainly didn't want anyone to get shot. "Put that thing away, Dan. Let's talk this through like rational people."

He shifted his gaze to meet Maggie's eyes, but kept his gun pointed at Jack. Who was now behind Maggie. Alarm bells in her head turned up to a near-deafening volume. Why did she get in the way of a bullet? The look in Dan's eye said he was prepared to shoot someone.

"He's lying to you, Maggie. You have to trust me. Cameron told me to take care of you. I know what's best for you." His calm tone begged her to believe him. "We need to get rid of him, and then you're going to help me find that book."

She held her hands out in front of her, palms forward, eyes focused on the gun, hoping like hell that Jack really was a cop and had some state trooper trick up his sleeve that could diffuse this stand-off. "Okay, no problem. I'll ask this guy to leave and then we can search together. You can tell me what the book looks like."

Dan's calm veneer cracked a bit, his brittle laugh on the edge of manic. "If I knew that I wouldn't need your fucking help. And no, genius, we can't let him *leave*. Both of you should come upstairs. Now." He motioned at Jack with the gun to include him.

Maggie stood rooted to the spot. "Dan, put the gun away. Think of your career. Think of your future."

He took a step closer, down another stair. A crazed gleam lit his eyes. "Are you not listening to me? I have no future unless I find that ledger. Now get up these *fucking* stairs and help me go through your *fucking* stuff."

Behind her, Jack's solid presence radiated heat and strength. She took a deep breath, drawing courage from his masculine scent, and tried one more time to talk sense into Dan. "Put the gun away before someone gets hurt. No harm, no foul." While she spoke, Jack slid one arm around her waist and pull her back against him, his hard chest grazing against her back.

Oh fucking hell, was she wrong about Jack? Was he actually the bad guy and Dan really was trying to protect her?

Jack's hot breath blew through her hair. Two whispered

words, barely loud enough for her to hear. *"Get out."* He pulled her to one side of him and deftly stepped in between her and the gun. Leaving her staring at the sea of flannel covering his large, solid back.

In Jack's left hand was another gun.

"Lower your weapon, Koslov." Jack's low voice skittered across her skin. He aimed his weapon at Dan, two hands holding it firm and steady. Somehow she couldn't picture pretty-boy-Dan actually firing a gun. But this guy, Jack? Yeah, he looked like he knew what he was doing.

All of a sudden things were very real.

And Dan was… laughing?

"Go ahead, tough guy. Shoot me. At this rate, I'm dead anyway." Dan waved his handgun in the air around his head with reckless abandon, but that gleam remained in his eyes. Maggie didn't believe for a moment that he was giving himself up and neither did Jack, who hadn't changed his protective stance.

"Lower your weapon," Jack repeated. "We can't discuss anything with guns drawn."

Noise behind her drew Maggie's attention. The front door swung wide to reveal her three roommates, Jasmine in the lead. Jas took one look at the gun in Jack's hands and screamed, shoving Tasha and Crystal back out of the door.

Gunfire exploded, Jack shoving Maggie down onto the floor so hard her shoulder nearly cracked as bullets whizzed through the room. Dan charged down the last few stairs and ran for the open door and out into the street.

"Are you okay?" Jack's graveled voice spoke directly in her ear, sending shivers across her skin. Or maybe the shivers were from being shot at. *Dan fired a gun at me! In my apartment!* She closed her eyes and tried to catch her breath, once again inhaling Jack's woodsy scent. *Focus on breathing. Deep breath in, exhale slowly.*

"Maggie, open your eyes. Answer me. Are you hit? Are you okay? I told you to get out of here, you should've listened." He'd rolled to the side, frantically patting down her shoulders and arms, looking for bullet wounds.

When she turned her head to follow the path of his hands, she saw her t-shirt was indeed spattered with thick splotches of blood. Funny, because she didn't feel like she'd been shot. As she started to tell him that, she saw that his flannel shirtsleeve was torn at the shoulder and also covered in blood.

"Jack, it's not me bleeding. It's you."

His hand went to his shoulder and he winced. "Guess you're right. Fuck." To her surprise, he looked relieved at the discovery. "I'm glad it was me and not you..." He was so close, those blue eyes staring straight into her soul, his hands cradling her face like she was something precious. Every spot where their bodies connected crackled with heat. A spark of awareness flashed between them, his lips one hot breath away from hers... and then he was gone.

Jack headed out the open door chasing Dan, giving orders as he ran. "Call 9-1-1. Tell them shots fired, suspect on the run."

As if in a daze, she stood and dug her cell out of her pocket, her lips tingling, her heart racing like a rocket headed for orbit. *Did all that really happen?* Dan shot at her. Jack almost kissed her.

She couldn't decide which of these things spiked her adrenaline more.

She shook her head and punched in the digits, still trying to understand what just happened, when the operator answered. "9-1-1, what's your emergency?"

9

*E*ven though Jack insisted he didn't need to be transported to the hospital, he was glad Maggie asked for an ambulance.

In Dan's rush out of the townhouse, Crystal fell down the stairs into the bushes. After a futile chase down the empty street, Jack returned to the scene and helped Maggie and her roommates extricate Crystal and her broken leg. The police and ambulance arrived minutes later, but the shooter was long gone.

Jack was glad he'd gone back to grab his gun from the glove compartment when Maggie first went upstairs. Who knows what might have happened otherwise? He got off two shots and told the police on the scene he'd tagged the other man in the leg. He knew he'd rushed his shot since his first instinct was to protect Maggie... and *holy shit*, sheer panic nearly paralyzed him when he saw the blood covering Maggie's shirt. His heart stopped when he saw the scarlet stains and her eyes closed.

Which didn't make a fuck-ton of sense, considering he

barely knew her and was only here to deliver the bad news about her sister. *A task he had yet to accomplish.*

The fact it was his own blood covering her shirt? Total relief, especially since he didn't yet feel the pain. Still too much adrenaline coursing through him from the confrontation. Well, and from the continued awareness of the beautiful woman seated next to him on the couch. The pain would come later. Of that he was sure. But first things first.

Find and arrest the asshole who shot at them.

And figure out why.

The EMTs made quick work of the scratch on his shoulder, where the bullet ripped through the flannel and grazed his deltoid before embedding itself in the far wall. No stitches required, although they'd cut the sleeve from his shirt in their haste to assess the damage. He refused to go with them to the hospital, insisting he needed to stay with Maggie and the investigation. The EMTs stabilized Crystal's leg before carting her off in the ambulance with Jasmine and Tasha following by car.

The cops confiscated Jack's weapon for evidence, which he wasn't too keen on. While they assured him that he could retrieve it at the station in a day or two, it meant a return trip to Worcester. It also meant he'd be without a gun until he got back to Cape Cod. Not a situation he wanted to be in with an active shooter on the loose.

After a grueling round of questioning for Maggie, she was told to wait on the couch with an icepack on her sore shoulder. While the team photographed the scene and dug stray bullets from the woodwork, Jack sat with her. His own bandaged shoulder started to ache but there was an even more uncomfortable task he still needed to accomplish.

"So you really are a state trooper," Maggie said, adjusting the icepack to a more comfortable position. "I wonder why Dan was convinced you were faking. I mean, he's a criminal defense lawyer. Shouldn't he know all you Boston cops by now? And I totally don't understand why he shot at us. None of this makes sense."

"How long have you known this lawyer guy?" The cops went through all this with her, but Jack was still curious. Why would Maggie trust someone like him?

She shrugged, then winced at the movement. He helped her adjust the icepack again. "Dan joined my sister's legal team a while back. Beginning of September maybe? When they moved Cameron to the hotel, he sort of got assigned as her bodyguard."

"Bodyguard? Then what was he doing in Worcester?"

Maggie frowned. "He said Cameron sent him to check on me." She folded one leg underneath her and turned to face him. "I haven't actually talked to my sister since I saw her last weekend in Boston. She snuck out of the hotel and we got our nails done and stayed at the brownstone overnight, watching chick flicks and ignoring his texts. Dan was super pissed when he found us. He showed up Sunday on the doorstep to drag her back to the hotel."

"So, not a very good bodyguard," Jack said with a smirk.

"In his defense, he's supposed to be a pretty good lawyer. Come to think of it, Dan was the one to answer her phone the last two times I tried to call. Both times he said Cameron went out and left her phone in the lawyer's office."

"If he's the designated bodyguard, why wasn't he with her?"

"I don't know."

"When were these phone calls?"

"Um, I called Friday from work when I was trying to figure out the schedule for next month, and then again last night after the break in. Why?"

Jack knew Cameron didn't leave her phone at the office "last night." She was already dead in the morgue at that point. "Maggie, Dan's lying to you. There's something we really need to talk about. About Cameron." He felt a shiver run through her body at the mention of her sister's name. Or maybe it was a chill from the ice. He put his arm around her to rub her arm, attempting to dispel the cold.

"Something bad happened to Cameron." The words came out as a whisper and he hugged her a little bit closer.

"Yeah, that's what I drove up from the Cape to tell you."

Maggie's face screwed up in confusion. "The Cape? I thought maybe you drove in from Boston. What's my sister doing on Cape Cod?"

"Maggie... your sister was found dead. The Medical Examiner positively identified her this morning, and sent me to inform you as the next of kin. I'm supposed to offer you a ride down to Bourne to ID the body."

"Cameron is... dead? How?"

"Drug overdose." He saw no reason to sugarcoat the facts. He watched her reaction, her face contorting with confusion.

"Drugs? Cameron didn't even smoke pot, let only touch the hard stuff. She drank wine, sometimes vodka." Her frown deepened as she pushed his arm off her shoulder, shifting away to face him. "No, I don't believe it. She can't be dead."

In Jack's experience, this was one of the most common responses when he delivered this type of news. The other two were either blind hysteria or an eerie zombie-like acceptance. Denial like Maggie's was probably the most common response, and the most easily dealt with.

"That's why I came to get you. To identify the body."

She stared back at him for what felt like forever before

taking a deep breath. "I need to change my shirt. This one's covered in your blood."

She left the room without another word.

He sat there, his own shirt torn and bloody, pushing away the conflicting information about the lawyer, and instead focusing on the kiss he almost stole earlier. What had he been thinking? Those few seconds of hesitation gave Koslov time to hightail it down the street, enough time to escape. Granted, he'd probably had a vehicle waiting close by, but still. If Jack hadn't hesitated, he might have caught the guy. The police could have him in custody right now, instead of all this endless questioning and speculation.

What the fuck possessed him to even consider kissing Maggie? He'd been overjoyed to realize Maggie was unharmed. The scratch on his own shoulder didn't bother him nearly as much as the thought of her being injured. Hell, this scratch was nothing compared to some of the hockey injuries he'd had in high school and college.

Which still didn't explain why he was still obsessing over his near-miss of a kiss. Thinking of how she felt underneath him. The way her breath fanned against his face and her heart beat an erratic tempo against his own pounding chest.

He needed to get a grip, and fast. This wasn't a date. She wasn't his to obsess over. She'd almost been the victim of a shooting, and her friend was on her way to the hospital, no thanks to Jack. Dr. Miller sent him for the dual purposes of informing her about Cameron, and keeping her safe.

So far, Jack had done a piss-poor job at both those things.

When Maggie returned wearing fresh clothes, cold fire burned in her eyes. He could tell she'd been stewing on the little bit of information he'd shared. And she was not satisfied with his answers. Even her voice was fiery as she spit her questions at him. "The police think this woman OD'd all on her own? They think my sister, Cameron Nelson, a successful and responsible business-woman, not to mention my only living relative, would decide to suddenly call it quits and check herself out in the middle of grand jury testimony? One more fallen soldier in the opioid army?"

"That's not what I said." Jack scrubbed fingers through his hair to keep from reaching to pull her back down onto the couch. He blew out a long breath. "Maggie, I'm on your side. The doc ruled it a suspicious death and asked me to bring you in."

"Bring me in?" Her eyes went even wider, her anger ratch-eting up a notch. "Am I a suspect or something?"

"No, no, of course not. Only…"

"I need to call her." Maggie pulled her cell phone from her pocket and clicked to her phone contacts. Watching the screen, Jack saw Cameron's name was the only one under "Favorites" at the top of her contact list. Not even her roommates made the cut, which told him the sisters were close. Sure, he and his brother Logan were close, but Jack had more favorites in his phone contacts than just his brother.

With two clicks, she'd dialed and held the phone to her ear. Her eyes met his. "It's ringing… It went to voice mail." After a beat, she left a quick message, even as the phone chimed with a notification.

Ending the call, she glanced at the display and grinned, before plopping onto the couch and turning the screen in his direction. "There, see? The body you found isn't my sister. She texted me back while I was leaving a message."

Jack read out loud. "In a meeting. Will call you later." He caught her eye. "You know that's one of those auto-replies, right?"

Her grin faded. "So? Someone swiped to send the message. It had to be my sister. Why would anyone else even bother to send a response?"

"Maggie, don't get your hopes too high. Dr. Miller seemed pretty sure about the identification." He left out the part about him being the one to discover the body, and how Maggie was a dead-ringer for the woman in the morgue, right down to the matching fingernail polish. He knew the truth from the moment she first opened the door.

The only difference between Maggie and the body on Dr. Miller's table was eye color. The rest? Identical in every way. If Jack didn't know any better, he'd swear he was sitting next to the ghost of the body he'd found on the side of Route 6.

A throat cleared. "Well, well, well. If it isn't the junior Beacon Hill Madam. Can't seem to stay away from trouble, I see." Jack looked up at the bulky cop who towered over Maggie, an unpleasant sneer on the guy's plump, doughy face.

Protective instincts roared through him and Jack jolted to his feet, feeling a deep sense of male satisfaction that he had several inches both in height and shoulder width on the other guy. "Back off, buddy. Maggie answered all the questions from your fellow officers. She's done until you capture the shooter. Or the thieves from last night's B-and-E. Or both."

Maggie gripped his shirt, trying to pull him back down to the couch. "Jack, it's okay."

Dough-face sneered in his direction, eyeballing the bloodied state of Jack's torn shirt. "I see someone wants to spend the night in lockup, *Jack-off.*"

Jack bristled at both the guy's tone and the slur. "On what charges?"

"Obstruction of justice, for starters," Dough-face said, narrowing his beady eyes to the point they practically disappeared behind his puffed out cheeks. "Wanna try me? C'mon, I dare you."

Maggie rose to her feet, putting both hands on Jack's chest. "Let it go, Jack. This jerk's not worth it."

"Yeah, *Jack-ass*, let it go." The cop obviously thought he was pretty original with his insults, laughing at his own joke.

Maggie's head whipped around. "Give it a rest, *Carl.* Jack's a state trooper who got shot in the line of duty, not a donut-obsessed beat cop whose sole purpose seems to be harassment."

Dough-faced Carl stood taller. "Hey, no need to get insulting, *Madam Nelson.* I'm just doing my job."

"Yeah? Do you have news about the break-in?"

"Uh, no. Nothing new."

"Then go *do your job* and leave us alone."

Carl opened his mouth to retort, but thought better of it and walked away, heading back to the kitchen and his fellow officers.

Jack looked down to find Maggie's hands still pressed against his chest even as she glared after the overweight cop. Her small fingers exerted enough pressure to let him know she was stronger than she looked. That she could hold her own. Gently, he circled her thin wrists in his hands, holding her in place rather than pushing her away. "Thanks for that. Here I thought I was protecting you, but I see you can fight your own battles."

She tilted her head to look him in the eyes, their deep forest color captivating him once again. "Creepy Carl had it coming."

His lips quirked at the alliterative nickname. "I take it you've run into him before?"

"Last night. After the break-in." She huffed out a breath and pulled her hands from his grasp. "Which according to Dan might not be random but related to the same ledger he was searching for." Her eyes widened. "Jack, my sister can't be the dead woman you found. Dan said Cameron sent him today. That she's busy working with the other lawyers on her testimony for tomorrow and couldn't leave Boston. He needs the notebook to help with her defense."

Jack's eyes searched hers, seeing the glimmer of hope rekindling. Not one to peddle false expectations, he shook his head. "Dan lied to you, Maggie. Judging from his actions today, it's more likely that Koslov is somehow connected to your sister's murder."

The word "murder" hit her like a physical blow, her head jerking back, her knees buckling as she dropped onto the couch. "I can't believe my sister might actually be... you know..."

"I know." He sat, his thigh pressed against hers, the heat from her body searing through him. His protective instincts flared again, wanting to pull her close and keep her safe, wishing to high heaven he wasn't here as the bearer of bad news. If he'd met Maggie under different circumstances...

But he didn't. He'd come to bring her to Cape Cod to identify a body. One that was most likely – *almost definitely* – her deceased sister. And now there was the added bonus of having a shooter on the loose who knew something about the murder and may or may not also be her sister's killer. Not the stuff to build a relationship on.

His timing was nothing if not awful.

He placed a hand on her knee and gave it a squeeze to get her attention. "Tell me what Dan said to you about this ledger. I noticed you didn't mention it to the cops."

She huffed out a sigh, relaxing slightly as he rubbed small circles on her knee. "I don't like to bring my sister into the conversation unless I need to. Things always get more... complicated when I do."

Judging by the attitude of the dough-faced cop, Jack figured Maggie earned the right to some privacy. But if this book was the whole reason Dan was in Worcester, he needed to ask and the cops should probably be informed. "Tell me what he said and I'll fill the detectives in."

Maggie tilted her head to one side. "He didn't say much, actually. He claimed she gave the book to me for safekeeping. But wouldn't I know if she gave me a notebook to hold for her?"

"Maybe. Maybe not."

"She did tell me there was a notebook. Her *little black book of vindication.*" Maggie dipped her head, cradling it in both hands. "Oh Cameron, what did you get yourself involved with?"

$\mathcal{M}$aggie closed the door on the last of the detectives. True to his word, Jack filled the detectives in on her sister's missing notebook, the possible motive for both last night's break-in and today's shooting.

Although she still felt confused about why Dan pulled a gun in the first place, she thought the confrontation and shooting were a misunderstanding. Dan obviously thought Jack was one of the bad guys. The ones Dan said wanted to keep the book out of the D.A.'s hands.

Yeah, nothing about today made a whole lot of sense.

Her roommates returned from the hospital, and after giving statements they closed themselves into Tasha's first floor room to fuss over Crystal and nurse their obvious hangovers from a long weekend of partying.

"It's okay to come out now," Maggie called down the hall. "Everyone's gone."

Crystal emerged on her crutches, Jas and Tash close on her heels, stopping short when they spied Jack sitting at the kitchen island. "Um, Maggie? One of them is still in the kitchen." Crystal flipped her long blonde hair in Jack's direction as Jasmine giggled behind her hand.

"The hot hunky one," Jasmine added in an excited stage whisper.

"Hey there, handsome." Tasha ran a hand along her own long tresses, neatly plaited in cornrows. "Thanks for saving our girl Maggie. She could use a strong guy like you in her life."

Maggie rolled her eyes even as her cheeks heated to inferno-like temperatures. Yeah, okay, Jack was the definition of sex-on-a-stick, like a romance novel hero or something, but that was no reason for everyone to fawn over the guy. Just because he was tall, dark and handsome with the chiseled body of a Greek god... and just because the almost-kiss they shared earlier was hotter than any actual kiss in her entire life... the thought stopped her cold.

How sad and pathetic is that?

If only Maggie met Jack under better circumstances. Sex with a guy like him would probably be off-the-charts hot. *Definitely sizzling...* But no. The sex-on-a-stick state trooper only showed up on her doorstep because a woman that might – or might not – be her sister was lying dead in a morgue somewhere on Cape Cod.

Which kind of took the heat out of the situation.

He was a law enforcement official doing his job. No more, no less.

Well, that last part wasn't quite true. He'd already protected her from a guy she'd thought was a friend, taking a bullet in the process.

Watching him banter back and forth with her roommates, she realized he wasn't that much older than she was, maybe a year or two. Yet he seemed like he totally had his shit together, with a responsible job and career path... while she still hadn't finished her undergraduate degree. Or decided what she wanted to do with her life, beyond getting out from under her sister's shadow.

"I'm starved," Crystal declared loudly. "Something about breaking a leg while being totally hungover makes a person extra hungry."

"I vote for pizza." Tasha pulled open a drawer to grab their collection of takeout menus. "But I could probably be talked into Chinese or Thai."

Maggie glanced at the clock on the kitchen wall. *Four o'clock? Where did the afternoon go?*

Jake pushed off from the counter and came toward her. "Maggie, I know it's getting late in the day, but I still think you should come down to the Cape with me. If we leave now we should be able to make it to Bourne by five thirty. Dr. Miller stays in his office until at least six most nights. I can call ahead to let him know we're on our way. If it's, uh, a wild goose chase, I can have you back here before eight o'clock tonight."

While her roommates were at the hospital, she and Jack discussed the pros and cons of letting the other women know the details of everything going on. Like the real reason Jack was here. Maggie firmly vetoed the idea because if they knew she was going with him to identify a body that might be her sister, they would all insist on coming along for support.

Bringing Dan and a shooting into their lives today – not to mention the break-in, if Dan was right and that was truly connected – was more than enough trouble for the three to swallow. No way did she want to talk with them about the drug overdose victim on Cape Cod who might or might not be her big sister.

Instead, she asked Jack to tell them it was a "police matter" related to the shooting that he wasn't at liberty to discuss. Maggie shrugged and told the girls she'd fill them in when she returned. Crystal took it in stride, still doped up on whatever pain meds the hospital had given her when they set the broken bone in her leg. Tasha and Jasmine held a whispered conference before pulling Maggie aside.

"You should bring your overnight bag, just in case," Tasha suggested with a wink.

"*Just in case?*" Jasmine looked offended. "Fuck that noise, make him buy you a lobster dinner on Cape Cod and then screw his brains out. You're doing the boy a favor, right? Helping with his investigation or whatever?"

"*Whatever* being the key phrase in that sentence." Tasha elbowed Maggie in the ribs and gave her another wink as Jasmine walked away. "It's been way too long since you've been out on a date, Mags. You need to exercise those muscles while you're young or they atrophy."

Again, inferno-levels of heat flooded her cheeks. "I'm not exactly sure what muscles you may be referring to, Tash, but…"

"Your dating muscles, nimrod. Jeez, I'm not the one suggesting casual sex. Although it doesn't sound like a bad idea…"

Maggie ignored the reference to sex. "Dating muscles? Is that a thing?"

Tasha laughed. "Depending on the guy, dating can most definitely count as hard work, so yeah, it takes muscle. And stamina. Then again if you want to skip the whole dating thing, wild monkey sex would work too for exercising muscles."

While Maggie's face bloomed with the heat of a thousand suns, Jasmine returned with an oversized sweatshirt in one hand and a canvas duffle in the other. She handed the sweatshirt to Jack. "I stole this from a frat party over the weekend. It

GHOST IN THE MACHINE

should fit and you're welcome to it, seeing how your shirt is kind of ruined."

He thanked her and gingerly pulled the black hoodie over his wounded shoulder, displaying the familiar Boston Bruins logo across his wide chest. Jas turned to Maggie and held out the duffle bag. "And this is for you, lady. I threw in a change of clothes and an extra pair of shoes, along with your toothbrush. You're ready for anything." She paired the last sentence with an exaggerated wink.

Maggie eyed the bag. It was the same L.L. Bean bag she'd used the week before when she took the bus into Boston to stay overnight with Cameron at the brownstone. *Was that just last week?* Maggie blew out a long, shaky breath. If Jack was right, she was on her way to the Cape to see her sister again.

She hoped like hell he was wrong.

Grabbing the bag, she leaned in to give Jasmine a quick hug. "Thanks. I'm sure I won't need it, but... thanks."

Jas picked up on the underlying tension and tightened the embrace. "Don't rush back. Crystal will be fine, and she totally doesn't blame you that she fell. That asshat clearly pushed her over the railing."

"Yeah, but..."

"But nothing, girlfriend. And listen, Tash and I will tackle the rest of the piles in the living room. By the time you get back here tomorrow, the place will be back to normal. Like nothing ever happened."

Tears pricked the backs of her eyes as Maggie gave Jasmine a smile and another quick hug. As much as she'd like to believe her friend's words, she knew they weren't true.

Things weren't going back to normal any time soon.

95

11

Somewhere along Route 495 South

$\mathcal{M}$aggie watched trees rush by the truck window as they raced down the highway. The fall foliage colors were already beginning to fade from their bright oranges, yellows, and reds to more muted tones, interspersed with shades of brown. The television weatherman promised peak foliage for the long weekend, but Maggie suspected "peak" lay further north, in the mountains of New Hampshire and Vermont.

She remembered spending long Columbus Day weekends with her parents, when she and Cameron were still in grade school, driving up into those same mountains for glorious weekends of "leaf peeping" and harvest fairs. Farmers' markets and craft shows and antiquing filled their days, along with laughter and togetherness. Autumn was her mother's favorite season, and she never failed to find some new place with brilliant foliage for the family to explore. Until Cameron went off to college, and then the long fall weekends were spent closer to home, driving across the river into Cambridge for parents' weekends at Harvard, along with homecoming festivities, Crimson football games and crew regattas along the banks of the Charles River.

Beautiful, brightly colored memories flitted through Maggie's brain in rapid succession as she stared unseeingly out the passenger window. The happy memories crowded out more recent events, like today's shooting in her townhouse, or last night's break-in. Or the fact that the state trooper in the driver's seat thought her older sister lay dead in a Cape Cod morgue.

Memories of deep red leaves and swaths of brilliant yellows faded into the past. Here in the present, along the highways of Southern Massachusetts, the leaves were falling, the trees already in their long, slow slide toward the starkness of winter. The season of death.

She wondered for the millionth time why she'd agreed to accompany Jack to identify the body in Bourne. *The body. Not Cameron.* It couldn't be Cameron. So why was Maggie in this truck, driving down this highway to see a body, a woman, who was definitely *not* going to be her sister?

When Jack held out a hand and his graveled voice told her to come along, she grabbed onto him like she was drowning and he was a life preserver. Perhaps her roommate Tasha had a point. If she was going to jump at the first hot guy to appear on her doorstep, Maggie certainly needed to get out on a few more dates. Although, when was the last time she'd run into a guy who had such an immediate and visceral effect on her? *Never.* She'd never felt drawn to anyone with quite the same intensity as when she opened the door and found Jack staring at her with those true-blue eyes of his.

A whispering voice in her head intruded on her thoughts of red maple leaves and true blue eyes, reminding her of the uneasy feelings she'd had about her sister all morning. All weekend. She knew in her bones something bad happened. Dan's arrival this morning only served to deepen her anxiety for her sister.

Maggie tried again to shrug off the uncomfortable feelings.

It's not Cameron. It couldn't be. Cameron was the only family she had left in the world. She couldn't be dead. *She can't be gone.*

Jack tuned the radio to a classic rock station, and Led Zeppelin crooned about buying a stairway to heaven. *Talk about ironic.* She glanced at Jack's profile, chiseled and strong, all cheekbones and jutting jawline, his fingers tapping the steering wheel along with the bass line. Her fingers itched for a set of drawing pencils and a sketchbook, but she clenched them into tight fists instead.

He caught her staring. "What? You okay?"

She shrugged. "I suddenly realized I'm in a car with a complete stranger going god-knows-where. If my mom was alive she'd be wagging a finger at me with that *I-taught-you-better* look on her face."

He chuckled. "You're safe with me, Margaret Nelson. I'm a sworn officer of the fine state of Massachusetts. And hey, we've already been through one, uh, situation together."

"Where you took a bullet for me." She sighed, remembering that she probably owed him her life. Who knows what Dan would've done if Jack hadn't shown up on her doorstep?

The side glance he gave her spoke volumes, if only she knew how to interpret it. "I know it's been a long day already, but I'm afraid it's not going to get any easier."

She tilted her head, assessing him. "I can't explain why Dan behaved the way he did, but it's not my sister at the morgue. It can't be." Even if her gut told her something was wrong it couldn't be that bad. *Cameron can't be dead. She wouldn't leave me all alone.*

Jack didn't answer for several long moments. Finally he huffed out a long breath. "Maybe we should talk a bit about what went down with Koslov. What exactly did he say when you called him last night for help with the break-in?"

Was Jack jealous? Something about the way his lips curled when he said Dan's name made her think maybe he was. Warm tendrils curled through her belly at the thought that Jack wanted to be the only one to protect her. The only one she called when she needed help.

"First of all, I did not call Dan. I dialed Cameron's number, and Dan answered. He told me she left her phone with him when she went back to the hotel for the night."

Which she hadn't found strange at the time, rattled as she was by the both the break-in and Creepy Carl's mere presence. But thinking it over now, in the fading light of day, it did seem kind of suspicious. Cameron never went anywhere without her phone. And now it happened twice in the last few days.

Dan answered Cam's phone on Friday too, when Maggie called from the diner about calendars and schedules for Thanksgiving break. She'd been trying to determine if Cameron wanted her in Boston for the week, if the trial would allow for a holiday break, or if she should stay in Worcester and pick up the extra shifts.

Jack's voice interrupted her musings. "Why was she staying in a hotel? Didn't you mention staying with her at her house last weekend?"

"My parents' house. Well, my house. They left the business

to Cam and the house to me. It's in an irrevocable trust. The state couldn't seize it when they shut down Cam's business." Which was totally beside the point. *Focus, Maggie.* She cleared her throat. "Yeah, her attorney moved her out of the brownstone and into a hotel closer to the courthouse after news leaked about the grand jury hearings. All the attention died down for a while, but the Assistant D.A.'s press conference stirred it all back up again. I'd like to give that woman a piece of my mind."

Another side glance from Jack, this one filled with a different sort of concern. "Didn't you hear the news today?"

"What news?"

"Monica Kazinski was found dead in her condo last night. Your sister's wanted in Boston for questioning."

Maggie's mouth fell open. She'd thought things couldn't get worse. Then it dawned on her. "Wait, if you think Cameron murdered that lawyer last night, how can she be in a Cape Cod morgue?"

Jack shook his head. "Maggie, I don't think your sister murdered anyone. I think she was probably a good person, caught up in some bad business."

"I know she wasn't innocent," Maggie blurted. "I know the spa offered more than manicures and massages."

Jack looked uneasy at the direction of the conversation. "I still don't think she murdered the A.D.A."

"I don't think she murdered anyone either. At least we agree on something." Maggie stared out the side window at the passing trees, deliberately avoiding the look of pity on Jack's face. She knew her sister did illegal things with her day spa, but murder? The Cameron she knew wasn't capable of hurting anyone. And as much as she kept telling herself Jack and his coroner were wrong about the body's identity, it was obvious

Jack believed Cameron was dead. His rock-solid conviction was beginning to chip away at her confidence. Well that, and the whispering voice in her head. The one that wouldn't shut up.

Finally she huffed out a breath and turned back to face him. "I know I said it before, but it occurs to me that you're *still* practically a stranger. Tell me something about yourself."

His startled look slid into an easy smile, telling her this wasn't what he expected from her. "What do you want to know?"

"Where did you grow up?"

"On the Cape. In Chatham."

"I didn't think anyone actually, you know, *lived* in Chatham."

"It's mostly summer people and tourists, but yeah, we have a year round population. It's not just me and my family."

She paused for a moment, considering his words. Did family mean wife? Kids? "You have family in Chatham?"

He nodded, his lips quirking up to one side in an adorable half-grin. "My parents still live in town. Actually, they own a bed and breakfast, taking advantage of the fact that Chatham is a tourist destination. I have one younger brother, Logan, but my dad has three older brothers. When they were in their twenties, Dad and my uncles came over from Scotland together to work for the summer."

"And never left."

A full-on grin lit his entire face, making her insides do a little shimmy of anticipation. "Nope. They all got married and stayed on Cape Cod. My dad and uncles are close. I'm one of eight cousins. We all grew up together in Chatham, and sometimes it feels like I have seven brothers instead of just the one."

"Eight of you, wow. Do they all still live there? In Chatham?"

Jack shook his head. "Logan does, and a few of the others, but some have scattered. Boston. New York. St. Louis. London.

Actually, this spring my cousin Dylan quit his fancy international finance job and moved home. He and another cousin are opening a bar in town."

"You're not all in law enforcement?"

He laughed. "Not at all. My cousin Ed is a detective in Chatham, but the rest of them followed other dreams. Makes it more interesting when we get together, I guess. The last time we were all in the same place at the same time was for a funeral. Ed's wife died of cancer a few years back."

"I'm sorry," she said automatically. "Cancer sucks."

"That it does," Jack agreed. "They're all supposed to come back to Chatham again this December for my cousin Quinn's wedding, so at least that's a happier occasion. You know, if you believe in wedded bliss and happily ever afters."

"You don't?"

He gave her another of those side glances and half smiles. "I haven't ruled it out, but I haven't met the right woman."

"No wife or girlfriend waiting at home for you?" There, she'd come right out and asked. *Tasha would be so proud.*

"Nope. My brother and I bought a house together that we're fixing up. Logan works for my uncle's construction company. He's doing most of the work himself. I'm just the hired muscle. He tells me what to do and I do it."

"Hired muscle?"

He laughed out loud this time. "Unpaid, of course. It's my house too, after all. Hoping to have a few more rooms finished before the rest of the cousins descend on the Cape for Quinn's wedding. Logan promised we'd put up a few of them in guest rooms or something, and now we need to actually finish them."

Maggie stared straight ahead, considering his large family and feeling a pang of jealousy. "My parents were both only children. My grandparents all died when I was very young. My parents died in a car crash ten years ago. Cameron is the only family I have left."

Jack reached over and squeezed her shoulder. "Maggie, I'm sorry."

"It's not her."

Jack returned his hand to the steering wheel without a reply.

"It's not her," Maggie repeated, almost daring him to contradict her statement.

She saw his jaw muscles clench, but his eyes remained on the road. And he remained silent.

Sunday, October 13, 5:45 p.m.
Barnstable County Medical Examiner and Coroner's office, Bourne

*H*eavy traffic in the other direction made Jack thankful he was pulling off the highway in Bourne. No way did he want to navigate either of the bridges onto Cape Cod amidst the crush of late day traffic he saw crawling in the opposite direction. Weekend visitors making their way back up to their homes in Boston and the suburbs around the city. Columbus Day weekend was the last hurrah for many of the small businesses on Cape who depended on tourists, including his parents B&B.

They'd made great time from Worcester, reaching the county offices before the doctor's six o'clock deadline. *"If I'm not home for dinner by six thirty, Myrna will have my hide,"* Sam Miller told him over the phone. *"Think you can make it back here in time, or do you have some allergic reaction to driving over the speed limit?"*

Speed limits existed for safety reasons, but Jack didn't argue the point with the man. After being shot at earlier, he had adrenaline to spare and needed a distraction. Driving fast helped distract him from the woman in the passenger seat.

The woman who hadn't spoken a single word to him in the last hour.

Pulling up and parking in front of the brick government building, he finally broke the thick silence. "We're here. Let's get this over with."

Her eyes met his for the briefest of moments before sliding away, staring out the windshield again while she nodded her agreement. Her hands clenched in her lap, her knuckles turning white.

Unlatching his seatbelt, he reached over to lay his warm hand on top of her cold ones. He felt the tremble in her fingers. He wanted to reassure her, tell her it was all going to be okay, but that would be a lie. Inside the building, her sister – her only living relative – lay dead in one of Dr. Miller's slide-out drawers. Tears brimmed in her eyes, threatening to spill.

"Maggie…" He was no good with tears. He had no idea what to say that might be of comfort.

She sucked in a deep breath and disentangled her hands from under his. She scrubbed the back of one hand across her eyes, swiping the errant moisture. "Let's get this over with," she said, her voice hoarse as she repeated his words back to him.

He nodded, giving her shoulder a squeeze before climbing out of the truck. Before he could get around to the passenger side to help her out of the vehicle, she was standing on the sidewalk staring up at the three-story brick building.

"Barnstable County Health Offices." She cleared her throat.

"Seems strange to have a morgue at a 'health' facility. Like they can make the corpses healthier or something."

"Death is a part of life," Jack commented. "They have morgues at hospitals too."

She grimaced. "I know. I was trying to make a joke. Trying, but failing miserably."

He stood next to her. "Maggie, it's okay to be upset."

"It's really my sister in there." It was a statement, not a question.

Jack nodded. He added a bit of information he'd withheld earlier, back when she was so far in denial it wouldn't have made a difference. "Her fingerprints are in the system from her arrest. They came back as a positive match."

She nodded her head once, a curt bob of acknowledgement.

"But ultimately, that's why you're here. To identify her."

"Right. I know that." She stared at the glass doors leading into the facility but didn't move forward. Instead, she wrapped her arms around herself as if unsure how to proceed.

This he could handle. Gently, Jack placed an arm around her shoulders and drew her against his side, marveling for a moment at how perfectly they fit together. Like the missing piece of a puzzle sliding into place. In that moment he realized he hadn't ever wanted a woman as much as he wanted Maggie. To hold, to comfort, to protect, to cherish, *to kiss, to ravish...*

He pushed the stray thoughts aside to focus on the here and now. Maggie needed his comfort, nothing more. Not now.

Fuck.

This sort of unprofessional behavior never happened to him. *Not ever.* At the very fucking least, he shouldn't be thinking about kissing her here on the sidewalk in front of the morgue. What kind of asshole did it make him if he couldn't comfort a woman without wanting to kiss her senseless? *Not any woman. Maggie.* There was something about her that called to him.

Maggie rested her head on his shoulder for a moment and her vanilla and lavender scent filled his senses. His eyes slipped closed as he inhaled. That smell had been driving him crazy for the last two hours along the highway, innocent and yet sensual.

She shuddered against him as she took a deep breath, but the trembling in her limbs quickly dissipated. "Okay. I can do this," she said, her voice low and determined.

He led her inside, his arm wrapped around her shoulders like it belonged there. They stopped to have a brief word with the receptionist, who was in the process of shutting her computer down and closing things up for the evening. She phoned Dr. Miller's office while they waited, and let him know *the sister* had arrived to view *the body*. When Natalie hung up the phone she gave Maggie a smile filled with long-practiced and very clinical sympathy before turning to Jack. "The doctor has the body in Viewing Room One."

He led Maggie to the elevator, exiting at the basement level and guiding her down the long empty hallway. Two viewing rooms were connected to the main autopsy suite, with mini-blinds in the windows facing the hallway, closing off the view. Jack knew that with cases where the bodies might be compromised in some fashion, the families could stand in the hallway and the blinds would be raised for viewing. A small comfort to grieving families, not having all of their senses overwhelmed at once.

Outside the door to Room One, Jack stopped and turned to face Maggie. Placing one hand on each shoulder, he looked into her eyes. "No matter what happens next, I'm here with you. You're not alone."

Her smile was sad but genuine. "You're a good guy, Jack."

"What do you need me to do?"

"I know it's not a trooper official duty or anything, but can you hold my hand? Is that allowed?"

He took her hand and gave it a hard squeeze before interlacing their fingers. "Whatever you need from me, Maggie Nelson."

"Thanks." Her voice sounded small, uncertain. All Jack wanted to do was wrap his arms tight around her and whisk her away from the sadness.

Instead, he took a deep breath, looking her in the eyes. "Ready?"

When she nodded in return, he pushed open the door to the viewing room. Sam Miller stood next to one of his wheeled tables, the body covered by a white sheet from the neck down.

Jack was struck again by the uncanny physical resemblance between the dead woman and the girl by his side. The similarity was remarkable, as if they were twins instead of merely sisters. There was no denying the relation between the two.

He glanced down to gauge her reaction and watched as Maggie's face drained of color. Her knees crumpled beneath her, leaving barely enough time for him to catch her.

"Shock, she must be in shock," he mumbled, trying to ease her unconscious form into a comfortable position on the hard cement floor. Quickly pressing two fingers to her throat, he found her pulse, relieved to feel it pumping at a steady rate. He looked up at the doctor and saw that he also looked unusually pale and frozen in place.

"What the hell happened? Is this normal?"

His words seemed to jolt the doctor out of his fugue state. "Nothing about this case is normal," he snapped. "What do you mean bringing her here is a mistake? You're the one who told me to send Jack to Worcester!"

Slowly, Jack rose to his feet, his brows furrowing with confusion. Quickly, he looked around the small viewing room, making sure no one else joined them while he'd been focused on Maggie. "Doc? Who are you talking to? I'm Jack, I'm right here."

"What do you mean she can see you?" The agitated doctor raised his hands to cover his ears. "How is this my fault? No, he doesn't know. Stop yelling at me!"

Okay, clearly Sam Miller is losing his shit. Jack held up his hands in a gesture of surrender. He stepped forward, for the second time in the same day placing himself between Maggie and a guy who was not thinking clearly and might be dangerous. *At least this one doesn't have a gun.* "I'm not yelling, Sam. Tell me what's going on. How can I help?"

He watched the other man close his eyes and shake his head as if to clear it, before slowly lowering his hands. He seemed aware of Maggie's prone body as if seeing it for the first time. "Jack is she okay? Did she hurt herself when she fell? I should check her for injuries."

Jack took a wider stance and stood his ground in front of Maggie. "She'll be fine, Doc. You stay where you are and explain what's going on."

The guy had the nerve to crack a smile. "And here I was, worried that you'd figured out my secrets long ago."

"You're scaring me, Doc. Tell me who's yelling at you?"

"Cameron. She's upset now because her sister can see her."

Maybe the guy worked down in this basement for too many years. Jack spoke slowly, enunciating. "Cameron Nelson is dead. I'm looking at her, right there on the table. She didn't say anything."

Sam turned his head, following Jack's gaze, before rolling his eyes as if Jack was the crazy one. "I meant Cameron's ghost, of course. The ghost is worried because she realized her sister can see her."

"Her… what?" Jack's eyes flicked over to where Cameron Nelson lay unmoving on the table.

"Ghost." The doctor closed his eyes briefly before rolling his shoulders back and standing taller. "I'm what some might call a psychic. I can hear ghosts."

Jack realized his mouth hung open and closed it. The doctor had definitely been stuck in this morgue for way too long if he thought he could speak with dead people. He needed to get Maggie out of here and call someone to help poor Sam Miller. He glanced around the room, looking for something to use in defense if the delusions worsened. *Too bad the Smith & Wesson was held for evidence back in Worcester.*

Sam crossed his arms over his chest, raising one eyebrow. "I'm not crazy, Jack."

"You're acting kind of crazy, Sam." Jack kept his eyes on the other man as he bent to lift an unconscious Maggie, hefting her into his arms without much effort.

"Jack…"

"Listen, why don't Maggie and I come back tomorrow? After you've had a chance to rest? We can go through the positive identification process then. Sound good to you?" As he spoke, Jack stepped backwards toward the door. The one that led to the hallway.

"Jack, wait…"

"No, Doc. We're out of here. I'll ask Natalie at the front desk to call Myrna for you, to come pick you up. I think you've inhaled too much formaldehyde or…or something today."

"Jack, really, if we could talk for a few minutes…"

He leaned his backside into the safety bar, pushing the door open behind him. "You stay there with the ghosts, Doc. I'll send someone to help you." When the door swung shut, Jack sprinted for the stairwell, not planning to wait for the elevator. Maggie remained silent and unconscious as he made his way up the one flight to the main entrance. The place was empty, Natalie already gone for the day. *Now what?*

In his arms, Maggie began to stir. "Jack? What... what happened?" Her free arm reached up and curled around his neck. Those forest green eyes gazed up at him with absolute trust, making Jack's heart stutter. It was like his name spilling from her lips erased all the weirdness he'd witnessed in the morgue.

"You fainted," he told her, voice husky, more gentle than he thought possible given the circumstances. She squirmed in his arms and he released her legs, letting them slide down against him to plant on the floor while he kept her upper body in a firm hold, her rapid breaths pressing her chest against his, the feel of her breasts distracting him from the problem at hand. *Get a grip, Jack.* "How are you feeling now?"

"I'm okay," she said, her voice breathy in a way that made his heart beat ten times faster. "Where are we? Where is my sister?"

"Maggie..."

"She was here, Jack. I saw her." Her eyes were wide green forests. He could get lost in eyes like those. *Shit.* He already felt like he was getting lost.

"Maggie, you did see her. Lying on the viewing table. Your sister is dead." He tried to make the words as gentle as possible, but nothing was gentle about their current circumstances.

She took a step back, out of his embrace. "You don't under-stand, Jack..."

He speared both hands through his hair. "You're right. I don't understand how Dr. Miller can believe in ghosts and stand there trying to convince me that he can talk to the dead.

He needs help. We need to get out of here and call someone to help him. His wife maybe? Myrna may know what to do to calm him. Bring him back to reality."

She shook her head. "He's telling the truth. I *saw* her. Just like I saw my mom after the car crash."

His entire body stilled. "What do you mean?"

"Her ghost. I saw her ghost."

"Ghost?"

"We need to go back."

13

ell, that was unexpected.

Her sister could see her. Actually *see* her. It seemed to have surprised the hell out of her as well, given the way Maggie fainted and passed out cold. But Cameron *should* have expected it, despite the fact she never believed the story about the visit from their mother's ghost. Ten years before, Maggie claimed she saw their mother's crying ghost. In retrospect the ghost story didn't seem as farfetched. Now that Cameron had first-hand knowledge that ghosts were real.

What did surprise Cameron was the memories flooding back to her, like a bolt of lightning striking her brain and setting it on fire. The minute she saw Maggie's face, she suddenly and without warning remembered every detail of her former life... the good, the bad, and the downright ugly.

She remembered leaving the law office with Dan to grab dinner, arguing on the phone with the Assistant D.A. about the encrypted files she'd dropped off earlier in the day. Something stung the back of her arm and suddenly the world was spinning. She found herself pushed her into the backseat of a strange car which drove her god-knows where, unable to control her arms or legs, unable to speak coherently. Trapped inside her own body, and as much as she tried to struggle nothing seemed to make a difference.

At some point she passed out. When she woke, her wrists and ankles were zip-tied to a chair while some Slavic-looking scumbag with a thick accent pushed a needle into her arm, shooting fire into her veins that woke every muscle in her body all at the same time, dialing every pain receptor up to eleven before switching them off abruptly. It was as if she'd plummeted from a high cliff into a deep vat of thick gelatin, the world around her muffled and distorted to her ears and eyes and brain.

Another man stood somewhere in the shadows nearby, his face just out of range, asking questions about her business partners. About her customers. About her connection to Governor Plunkett. Incoherent words tumbled from her mouth of their own accord. She had no control over what she said or didn't say, feeling like she was floating somewhere nearby watching the scene unfold like she was watching a movie. A really, really horrible movie where she didn't want to see any more but she couldn't change the channel.

Until they'd given her one injection too many.

She remembered not being able to focus her eyes at all, and pressure like an elephant repeatedly stomping his enormous foot into her chest. The crushing pain made it harder and harder to draw air into her lungs, until she eventually forgot why she should even bother to try.

When she woke she was tumbling atop that garbage bag along the side of the highway.

Since that bag held her body, it meant she was already a ghost.

How they knew where to find her still puzzled her. She wondered what happened to Dan, whether he survived the attack. But neither of those things really mattered. All that mattered was keeping her little sister safe from those monsters.

Maggie was truly innocent.

Cameron wasn't.

A few years after her parents' accident she learned the business wasn't totally on the right side of the law. Meaning Cameron was already a criminal, complicit in the sex trafficking hidden behind the upscale façade.

Beacon Hill Beautiful was her father's business before she took over after his death. Turns out there was a whole second set of books that her dad's business partner Nikolas managed to keep secret. By the time she figured it out, it was too late and she was in too deep, her name and reputation intertwined with everything. The only thing she could do was to keep Maggie away from the darkness.

It wasn't until her arrest that things began to fully unravel, exposing an ugly underbelly Cameron could no longer pretend to ignore. The extra income wasn't only about illicit sex between consenting adults, but also corruption and bribery on Beacon Hill. Photos and video recordings of lawmakers and lobbyists in compromising positions, used to manipulate their actions and sway their votes by the shadowy influence peddlers Nikolas worked with. That her *father* had worked with. The *real* business partners, so to speak. *Beacon Hill Beautiful* was a miniscule cog in a very dark and dirty political machine. One with aspirations that reached well beyond the Massachusetts State House.

All Cameron wanted to do was keep her little sister safe.

In life she may have failed, but as a ghost she had a second chance. One she was determined to make the most of.

Lost in her memories for gods knew how long, Cameron became aware of her current surroundings again when Dr. Miller pulled the white sheet over her head and wheeled the table toward the exit. He was taking her body back to the morgue, to the shallow drawer scented with formaldehyde and antiseptic.

"Wait! Doesn't my sister need to come back and identify me?"

The doctor hung his head and sighed. "I'm not sure Jack will allow it."

"Why? What happened?"

His face scrunched up in puzzlement. "You were right here with me. Yelling at me."

"Yes but..." Cameron didn't know how to explain. Seeing her sister broke down the walls erected in her mind. She'd been drowning in her memories, oblivious to the real world. "I was busy... remembering."

He stopped moving toward the door. "How much did you remember?"

"Almost everything, I think. I need to talk to Maggie. She's in danger because of something I told the monsters who kidnapped and drugged me." They'd known so many details about the upcoming trial, about the names and details she planned to make public. Someone – either from the D.A.'s office or from her own legal team – must have leaked the information. And now, thanks to her over-drugged state, the bad guys knew she gave a copy to A.D.A. Kazinski... and another backup copy to Maggie.

The doctor shook his head, staring vaguely in the direction where she was standing. "Jack thinks I'm crazy. I tried to explain that I can hear you, talk to you, but he was having none of it. I'm sure they're long gone by now."

The last words were barely out of his mouth when the door to the hallway swung open, Maggie in the lead and pulling Jack along, their hands joined and fingers entwined. Maggie looked determined and Jack looked decidedly pissed off by the entire situation. He spoke first.

"Okay, Doc, start talking."

14

Maggie stared at the ghost of her sister, hovering next to the doctor. She wasn't sure what she should expected from a ghost, but her sister looked almost alive – dressed in one of those sleeveless designer sheaths she often wore, her hair loose, her makeup perfect as always. The only difference seemed to be that everything about her – dress, hair, skin tone – was muted into a faded color scheme, as if she were a filtered Instagram photo instead of a real person.

Which kind of made sense, seeing as how she was no longer a "real" person. At least not a live, corporeal one. Regardless of reality, her sister's ghost stared right back at her, tears brimming her eyes.

Jack squeezed her hand, reminding her of his solid presence by her side. "Doc, I don't believe in ghosts and don't understand what kind of game you're playing…"

Maggie cut off his words by pressing two fingers to his warm lips. She ignored the jolt that ran through her and focused on calming him. "It's okay, Jack. It's not a trick because

I can see Cameron's ghost standing right there next to Dr. Miller."

She pointed at her sister, and saw her mouth moving but couldn't make out what Cameron was trying to say. The sounds were more like low moans than actual words. She flashed back ten years to her mother's ghost appearing in her bedroom, the crying moans all she could hear. Had her mother been trying to talk to her as well? Trying to tell her something? Maggie listened to her sister without any comprehension, and watched Cameron become more and more frustrated.

She shifted her gaze to the doctor. "Can you understand what she's saying?"

He cocked his head, assessing her. "I can. And I take it you can see her ghost?"

"But I don't know what she's saying. It all sounds garbled."

Jack tightened his grip on her hand and she spared him a glance. His smile looked forced, his lips pressed tight. "Are you sure this is okay? Are you... okay?"

Maggie squeezed his hand and nodded. "Cameron's ghost is here with us."

Jack's eyes darted in the doctor's direction before zeroing back on Maggie's face. "I don't see anything. Or hear anything."

The doctor cleared his throat. "Maggie, your sister wants to apologize for dragging you into this mess. She says she tried to keep you separate from everything."

Watching her sister's mournful expression, Maggie's eyes filled with tears. "She sure did. We never talked about the business at all, and now I wish we had. I would've told her not to do it. We didn't need the money that bad. We could've sold the brownstone and moved to the suburbs or something."

"They wouldn't have allowed that, she says. Your father tied the business with them years ago."

Maggie frowned, her eyes darting between the doctor and Cameron's ghost. "What does Dad have to do with any of this?" She watched the doctor nod his head as he listened, absorbing Cameron's lengthy explanation. The longer she spoke, the more color leached from her body, her ghost becoming more and more translucent as the conversation continued. "Dr. Miller, Cameron looks like she's fading away. What's going on?"

He held up one finger, the gesture obviously intended to ask her to wait.

Jack's warm breath tickled her ear. "I gotta say, this is all kind of creepy. Not to mention, I feel pretty useless. Maybe I should go wait in the hall or something?"

She squeezed his hand again, trying to pretend that she was used to seeing ghosts and hearing their murmured whisperings. That it was A-Okay having a Medical Examiner as the conversational go-between with her sister. *Her dead sister.* She turned her head to look him in the eyes, intending to say something self-deprecating to let him know that no, he wasn't useless and this wasn't in any way normal. She needed him right here next to her, making her feel safe.

This close to him, though, their noses practically rubbing together, it was too tempting to press her lips to his and take a little taste of all that protective heat. To pretend nothing else was happening except for the electricity sparking between their bodies.

The stray thought shocked her, not used to her body being out of her control. Everything felt out of control at the moment, teetering on the brink of sanity. *Miles and miles from normal.*

Instead of stepping into all that heat, she drew back, pulling her hand away from Jack's and turning her head away. This was insane. Her sister's body was lying on the table not six feet away from her, her *sister's ghost* hovering on the other side of the room from her. She could feel a giant sob trying to rise up out of her chest but she clamped down on it hard. She needed to get a handle on her emotions. Or get her head examined. She had more important things to focus on right now than the hot hunk of a man by her side.

She glanced back at the doctor listening to her sister, watching as the last remnants of her sister's ghost faded away, dissolving to nothingness.

"Wait a minute, Dr. Miller! W-what happened to Cameron?" Maggie began to panic, her heart suddenly pounding too many beats per second. Had she missed her chance to get answers? To say anything meaningful to her sister? "W-where did she go? She can't leave me again!"

Dr. Miller held up both hands. "Now, now, no need to be alarmed. Strong emotions like this are taxing for the recently dead. Your sister needs to recharge."

"Recharge? Like a battery?" Jack's breath was hot against her skin as he stepped close behind her, placing his hands on her waist as if to anchor her. Moments ago she'd wanted to put distance between them, but now she welcomed his steadiness. She tried to slow her rapidly beating heart, focusing on the feel of Jack's fingers pressing into her hip bones.

"I think it's something along those lines." Dr. Miller shook his head as he lowered his hands, stuffing them into the pockets of his white lab coat. "Despite my ability to hear them speak, I don't understand much about the mechanics of the spirit world. I do know that the ghosts who talk to me have unfinished business."

"Like my sister," Maggie whispered in between focused breaths. *Inhale, two, three, four. Exhale, two, three, four.* Recharging. Not disappeared forever.

"Yes, like Cameron," agreed the doctor. "She'll be back tomorrow. You can come see her then. The lawyers from the D.A.'s office won't be here until Tuesday morning, as tomorrow is still a holiday."

"The D.A.?" Jack sounded puzzled. "Why not her own attorney?"

"The article we saw online about the hearing scheduled for this week. Thought I should call to let them know their star witness wouldn't be available," Dr. Miller explained. "Now, why don't you two go upstairs to the waiting room while I wheel this table back to the morgue? We should talk, but first I need to call Myrna and tell her I'll be late for dinner."

Jack slid his hands up and down her chilled arms, rubbing warmth back into them. She hadn't even realized how cold she was until she felt the heat radiating off his body. He spoke for both of them, since she couldn't find her voice. "That sounds like a fine idea, Doc. We'll meet you upstairs."

She allowed Jack to lead her out of the viewing room and back to the elevator. On the first floor, he steered her to an alcove with chairs and a couch. A vending machine in the corner gave off a soft, electronic buzz, the only sound in the otherwise empty building.

Pulling her down onto the couch, he wrapped an arm around her shoulders and Maggie felt the bruises from earlier in the day start to throb, reminding her she'd been shot at only a few hours before. By someone she thought she could trust. And now here she was, letting a guy she'd just met comfort her while she waited to hear what her dead sister's ghost needed to tell her.

Could her day get any stranger?

A shiver zipped through her body, from the cold or from the odd nature of the situation, she couldn't say. Jack held her against his side, letting his body heat warm her, calm her. He drew a deep breath and exhaled before speaking. "Not gonna lie. This whole thing has me shaken up. I mean, I'm not usually one to believe in ghosts. Not even this close to Halloween."

She huffed out a mirthless laugh, staring at the vending machine. Yeah, she could totally see that. "You seem like a black and white kind of guy." Which made all kinds of sense. He was a state trooper, after all. All about the letter of the law. And yet he was still here with her, taking care of her, comforting her. This wasn't his job. He was supposed to *notify the next of kin,* or whatever it was the trooper handbook stated for these sort of situations. There had to be a gold-embossed rule book filled with codes of conduct and whatnot. A hand-book Jack was sure to have memorized in its entirety because he seemed like that kind of guy. One who knew the rules and played by them.

Although…she was pretty sure his handbook of black-and-white rules didn't mention taking a bullet for that *next of kin,* or chauffeuring her halfway across the state, or rubbing her arms to dispel the chill she couldn't seem to shake.

His hand continued to stroke up and down her arm, the simple motion the only thing keeping her grounded. "When we studied Descartes in college, I was always on the side arguing against his dualistic concepts of body and mind being separate entities."

She stared at him, not understanding his train of thought. She found it hard to picture Jack taking philosophy classes, let alone connecting philosophical treatises with her dead sister. "What are you talking about?"

"Descartes thought the mind and body were independent, and wrote that the mind could exist independently of the actual brain matter. The spirit living on after death."

"Ghosts," she whispered, thinking of her sister's faded and shadowy presence in that white basement room.

"Ghosts." Jack sighed and shook his head. "I don't believe in them. I agreed with the philosophers like Gilbert Ryle, who said consciousness depends on having a body."

She leaned in closer, laying her head against his strong shoulder. "So how do you explain what's happening now with my sister?"

"I can't."

Her eyes suddenly burned with unshed tears. She squeezed them closed and focused on the feeling of his hand, timing her breathing along with his steady strokes. *Up, two, three, down, two, three.* When she opened them again, a black cat was sitting in the middle of the room, staring directly at her. Green eyes practically glowed in the dim light of the waiting room. *Another ghost? Or an omen of some kind?*

"Jack," she whispered. "Can you see that? Is it real?"

"You mean Marley? Yeah, he's real all right. He lives here."

"What, here? In the morgue building?"

"Yeah. The Doc jokes that since the cat was named after a ghost, it's fitting he lives here."

"Named for a ghost?"

"You know Dicken's Christmas Carol? Marley is the first ghost that visits Scrooge. The cat arrived with the name on his collar." Jack's hand continued the rhythmic strokes, her breathing now slowed and synced to the movement.

"Where did he come from?" The way the cat stared unblinking at her was kind of freaky. Solid black fur seemed to absorb the surrounding light. He sat without moving a muscle or even twitching an ear. Yet another shiver ran down her spine, but she found she couldn't look away.

"He kind of lives here, in the building." Jack must have felt the shiver, tucking her closer into his side, his warm hand now gently cupping the side of her head. She let out a sigh, feeling a little of the tension drain from her body as she listened to his gruff voice. If only she could bottle that voice to break it out when she was feeling anxious. She almost smiled at the thought.

"As the story goes, Marley came in with a body a few years back, riding along with the EMTs and staying after they left. His owner was an old man with no other family, and no one could coax the cat out of the morgue, away from the guy. Poor cat had nowhere else to go. So now he lives here, keeps an eye on the place. Gives Doc someone to talk to."

As Jack spoke, the cat's head turned to face him instead, and Maggie realized the glow she'd seen in the animal's eyes was not some supernatural menace but merely a reflection from the vending machine. "Seems like the doctor would have plenty of people to talk to even without the cat, if he converses with ghosts."

Jack drew in a sharp breath. She felt his body tense and realized how truly uncomfortable he was with the whole ghost-whispering thing. Shootings and bodies didn't faze him, but talking to ghosts? Seeing ghosts? Maggie guessed that didn't fit very well with his black and white view of the world.

"Sorry to keep you waiting."

They both looked up as Dr. Miller entered. Jack's arm dropped from her as he stood to greet the other man. The cat also stood and arched his back before sauntering toward the window and jumping up onto the ledge, as if wanting a better vantage point to watch the scene unfold. His black silhouette stood out against the window, outlined by the purple glow of twilight over the dark waters of the canal.

"Doc." Jack nodded to the other man and folded his arms across his broad chest. "I guess I owe you an apology for my earlier assumptions. It's just... well, this whole day has thrown me for a loop."

"Apology accepted. I've had quite a few years to come to terms with the existence of ghosts. I don't expect it's an easy thing to suddenly wrap your head around." The doctor crossed the room and took the seat in front of the window, facing Maggie.

"Why is my sister here, Dr. Miller? What happened?" Maggie hugged her arms around herself, feeling chilled without Jack's heat to keep her warm.

"Do you mean how did she die or why hasn't her spirit moved on?"

She swallowed the lump in her throat. *Dead.* Her sister was dead. "Jack said she overdosed?"

He nodded, his voice brisk and clinical. "Cameron Nelson died from an overdose of fentanyl in her bloodstream. All physical indicators point to homicide, whether intentional or not, as there are faint ligature markings on her wrists and ankles to indicate she may have been bound at the time of the injections. Exact time of death is hard to pinpoint. I'm suggesting a six-hour window spanning Friday night into Saturday morning."

He paused to look over at Jack before returning his focus to Maggie, his tone softening. "That's the gist of my official report. Unofficially, your sister told me she was snatched off the street on Thursday. Two men tied her to a chair and questioned her until the accidental overdose occurred. Because she was drugged, she's not sure exactly how much information she gave the kidnappers, but thinks she told them she gave a certain file to the Assistant District Attorney, and a copy to you for safe keeping. She's also pretty sure they searched the brownstone already without finding it."

Stunned, Maggie tried to absorb all the information, both

the official and the unofficial. The bottom line? Her sister was dead. But to find out Cameron was kidnapped and tortured added another layer of grief on top of the one she already struggled with. Her chest tightened with the effort to hold back her sobs. The tears that threatened earlier rolled down her cheeks, one after another.

Jack's voice filled the silence. "Someone definitely broke into Maggie's apartment last night, searching for something. The place was still a wreck when I arrived at noon."

Dr. Miller looked puzzled. "I thought you drove out to Worcester to pick Maggie up from college?"

"Yeah? So?"

"I'm sure Cameron said the brownstone is in Boston."

The brownstone was ransacked too? Why didn't anyone tell me? Maggie drew in a shaky breath. "You said the lawyers from the District Attorney's office are coming?"

The doctor nodded. "I called them once the fingerprints came back a positive match. Frankly, the only reason I sent Jack to Worcester was because your sister insisted upon it. She thought you might be in danger."

Maggie exchanged a look with Jack. If Jack hadn't arrived when he did to intervene with Dan, who knows where she'd be right now. She still wasn't totally convinced the lawyer was one of the bad guys, but if he was... Maggie could be tied up and drugged right this very minute. The thought sent ice water racing through her veins.

She tried to focus her attention on the doctor. "What version of events did you give the D.A.? Official or unofficial?"

Dr. Miller's lips quirked. "You mean, ghost or no ghost?"

She gave a sharp nod.

"I only relay official reports to law enforcement officials. Testimony from ghosts doesn't tend to hold up in court."

Her stomach knotted at his cavalier tone. *Testimony from ghosts.* Someone kidnapped and tortured her sister before dumping her body by the side of the road. The idea that it was inadmissible in court didn't change any of those facts.

Cameron was dead. There were no witnesses besides her ghost.

Someone was going to get away with murder.

Jack rubbed his hand along her spine, up and down in a gesture obviously meant to soothe. "Maggie. Are you okay?"

Maggie took a shaky breath. "What does it matter?" An anguished cry escaped with her words. "Cameron is dead. Someone kidnapped and killed my sister." Her shoulders heaved and she curled in on herself, folding her chest down against her knees as the sobs wracked her body and she gave herself over to sorrow.

15

*T*ears were his kryptonite.

Jack froze in place, unsure how to offer help or if she even wanted him to try. She'd been so strong all day long, while all he could do was think about kissing her. That spark of awareness he'd felt arcing between them only moments before now drowned in a pool of salty tears, and there wasn't a damn thing he could do about it. He needed to stay focused on the here and now.

Because he wasn't about to let anything happen to Maggie.

He looked Sam in the eye. "Is there anything else we need to talk about? Anything that won't wait until morning? Because otherwise I'm going to take Maggie somewhere to feed her and let her rest. She needs time to absorb all this information. To recharge, as you say, just like the ghost does."

Sam moved a step closer, lowering his voice to barely a whisper, anxiety lacing his words. "There are political heavy-weights looking for that notebook, Jack. I don't know what our governor has to do with operating a massage parlor, but Cameron thinks he's the reason she was kidnapped."

"Because of her notebook?"

Sam nodded. "These guys are serious about finding it first. They've already killed one woman..."

"Two, if you count the A.D.A., which I think we need to." He glanced back at Maggie, still curled into a fetal position on the couch.

Sam followed his gaze. "Does she know where the notebook is?"

"She says no."

"Do you believe her?"

Jack frowned. "Of course I do."

"Cameron said she gave it to Maggie." The doctor's eyes widened. "Actually, what she said was '*Maggie has the file.*' And what you're telling me is that Maggie *doesn't know* she has the file."

"Exactly. Maybe you can get your ghost to give you more details. What the book looks like, where she put it..." He realized how crazy that sounded. He was asking the doctor to get vital case information from a ghost. But what choice did he have? There was obviously something going on here that he couldn't explain, not in any way that made rational sense to him.

Could ghosts exist? Could Dr. Miller actually have psychic powers to talk to the recently dead? Did Maggie really see her sister's ghost down there in the morgue standing next to her own dead body? The last hour had certainly strained the parameters of what he believed to be true... Jack wasn't one hundred percent sure about anything at the moment. But he knew there was one positive thing he could do right now. He glanced back at Maggie on the couch. "I'm taking her home."

"Back to Worcester?"

"No. Back to my place. In Chatham."

16

Sunday, October 13, 8:07 p.m.
23 Crosswind Farm Road, Chatham, Massachusetts

*T*raffic on the Cape was light. As he turned onto the dirt driveway that lead to his house, Jack glanced over at the passenger seat. Maggie hadn't said a word for the last half hour, barely even acknowledging him when he led her out of the county building to his truck. He'd left her alone as she texted with her roommates to let them know she wouldn't be coming home. She also called her boss at the diner to let him know she had a family emergency and would be out of town for a few days. He was surprised by her dispassionate tone, and the fact she didn't tell him about her sister, but then again, maybe she wasn't ready to fully process everything that happened. He didn't know quite what to think. Or whether bringing her home was what he should do.

But it felt right.

Motion detector flood lights flicked on as he pulled his SUV next to his brother's tough-as-nails work truck, a brand spanking new F350 with all the bells and whistles. Not that he begrudged his little brother a new toy, not when business was going well. But Logan's shiny red truck seemed symbolic to Jack, as if it shouted to the world how Logan's life was racing along while Jack's was... not. He'd been in the same job now for four years, since graduating from the academy, and driving the same SUV for longer. Not that he cared about material things. He didn't. Not really. If he did, he wouldn't have dropped out of law school.

And why the fuck was he sitting in his driveway, stewing over stupid shit like whose truck was flashier? He had a grieving woman in the passenger seat in desperate need of food and sleep, and any other comfort he could offer. He wanted to help solve the mystery of her sister's missing notebook. Sam's warnings weighed heavily on his mind, especially as he'd already been shot at once today.

Most of all, he wanted to keep Maggie safe.

He shifted into park and saw her eyes were closed. When did she fall asleep? He reached over to brush a stray lock of dark hair from her face. A sigh escaped her lips and blew warmth across his hand. His heart squeezed tight in his chest. *God, she was beautiful.*

Long eyelashes fluttered open, green eyes sparkling under the glare from the outdoor lights. She looked out the windshield, into the cluster of scrub pines surrounding the house. "Where are we?"

"Chatham. My house, actually."

Cute little wrinkles lined her nose and forehead. "This is Cape Cod? But those are pine trees. Where's the ocean?"

Jack's lips quirked up. "Not everyone can afford beachfront property."

"That's not what I meant. But I thought, you know, Cape Cod…" A flush rose in her cheeks as she squirmed in her seat and sat a bit straighter, clearly embarrassed. The warm color highlighted how pale she'd been, ever since she first stepped foot into the morgue. A mere shadow of the vivacious beauty he'd met earlier in the day. Her complexion now matched that of the sister lying in the morgue, a depressing thought if there ever was one.

He cleared his throat of the unwanted emotions, pushing on the door handle. "No worries. I'll show you the beach in the morning. Right now, let's find you some dinner and a bed so you can rest."

"Dinner?" Maggie closed her car door as Jack rounded the front of the vehicle. She tugged on the straps of her canvas bag, repositioning it on her shoulder as her stomach let out a loud grumble. "I haven't eaten anything except coffee since yesterday's shift at the diner."

Jack smiled. "Coffee isn't actually a food group, you know."

"Bite your tongue!" Maggie speared him with a look of disapproval. "Coffee solves all life's problems in one delightful little cup."

His lips quirked in response. "Duly noted. It's Logan's night to cook. If you don't like whatever it is, I can run out and grab pizza. And coffee, if it's necessary. Although it might be better if you don't indulge in caffeine at this hour and actually get some sleep tonight."

Another growl from Maggie's stomach punctuated the stillness of the evening. "Your brother cooks? Wow, I haven't met him yet but I think I'm already in love. Or at least my stomach is."

Jack smiled and pressed his hand against her lower back, steering her toward the front path. She fell in step next to him, and for a moment Jack forgot all the circumstances leading up to this moment and reveled in the warmth of her presence, the rightness of having her by his side, the feeling of belonging with someone so bright and funny. *This. This is what I want.*

The front door swung open, his brother's hulking shape outlined by the bright lights behind him. "Finally! Where the fuck have you been, Jack? I expected you home from the fishing trip hours ago. What if I'd been counting on fish for dinner tonight?"

It took Logan a minute to realize Jack wasn't alone. His imposing form stepped forward, the porch lights casting shadows on his deepening frown. "Hello, who do we have here? Don't tell me you caught her out on Dylan's boat! Man, the one day I don't go fishing and you find actual mermaids!"

Maggie shrunk against Jack's side, clearly surprised by the sheer size of Logan. Well over six feet tall and built of muscle, Logan cast an impressive shadow. As the pair stepped further down the path and into the light streaming from the front door, Jack watched his brother's teasing expression morph into something more akin to interest. A wave of jealousy washed through Jack so fast he nearly stumbled. *Mine*, roared a voice in his head. He put a possessive arm around her shoulders and gave her what he hoped was a reassuring squeeze.

"Maggie, this big goofball is my *little* brother Logan. Lo, this is Maggie Nelson. She's helping me with a case and needed a place to stay for the night. I hope you made enough for three."

Logan's dark eyes ping ponged between Jack and Maggie, as if trying to discern the truth of the situation. Finally, his eyes settled on the girl, his lips quirking into a flirty smile. "You're in luck, Maggie Nelson. I cooked up a big ol' lasagna in case the fishermen came home emptyhanded. I was putting garlic bread in the oven when I saw Jack's headlights pull up the driveway."

As Logan spoke, the fragrant smells of tomatoes and garlic and Italian spices hit Jack's senses. His own stomach growled, almost as loudly as Maggie's. "Enough with the introductions. Let's eat."

ack watched Maggie push her chair back and rub her stomach. "That's it, Logan," she said with a groan of pleasure. "I'm officially in love with you."

Jealousy flashed through Jack like wildfire. Which was ridiculous. He tried to shake it off but the hot itch under his skin wouldn't go away. Meanwhile, Logan just laughed as he stood and began to gather the dirty dishes with his meaty paws. "Hasn't a guy ever cooked for you before, Mags?"

Mags. His brother had known Maggie for all of two hours and already had a nickname for her. Then again, he'd always been the more social of the brothers. Despite his towering height and imposing bulk, Logan had the good nature of a teddy bear and made friends wherever he went.

"You seriously underestimate your culinary super powers. That was the best lasagna I've ever had. Better than one of those Italian places in the North End." She picked up her plate and two of the empty beer bottles. "Let me help you clean the kitchen."

"No need for that," Jack said, pushing his chair back quickly. "You're our guest. Besides, it's my job to wash up on the nights my little brother graces us with his cooking." The words were out of his mouth before he saw his mistake.

Logan grinned at Maggie, spiking another shot of jealousy through Jack's veins. "Yeah, let the old man do the dishes. Let's go find something to watch on Netflix."

Old man. It struck him yet again that Logan and Maggie were about the same age. A thought that obviously occurred to Logan over the course of dinner, as they talked and determined they'd both graduated from high school the same year.

Old man. It's not like Jack was ancient, for fuck's sake. *Since when was twenty-nine over the hill?* But okay. It made sense that she'd be attracted to someone her own age. Feel more comfortable with someone easy-going like Logan, instead of an old cop with a stick up his butt. What was it she'd called him? *Black and white.* Which translated into *no fun at all.*

He rinsed the dishes and shoved them into the dishwasher with a little more force than necessary, before wrapping tinfoil over what was left in the casserole dish. The longer he stood in the kitchen, the more out of sorts he felt, listening to the shared laughter and murmurs coming from the living room. She seemed comfortable with Logan. Relaxed. Which was a good thing, Jack told himself. He brought her here for a bit of normal, after all. He just wished it was him in there making her laugh. Watching that spray of tiny crinkles form next to her eyes when she smiled. *Getting lost in those deep pools of green...*

He picked up the foil-wrapped casserole dish and stared at it for too long. He should probably scoop it out onto a plate and clean the baking dish with the tomato sauce and mozzarella oozing down the sides. His brother's laughter spilled out of the living room again and Jack's jaw clenched. Logan would probably take the leftovers for his lunch the next day, but he could fucking dish it into Tupperware by him-*fucking*-self in the morning. Jack pushed the dish onto the refrigerator shelf and slammed the door.

He eyed the rest of the mess on the counter by the stove and let out a hefty sigh. Dirty pans, bowls, knives and utensils sat haphazardly on the sauce-stained countertop, along with an assortment of cans and plastic containers that needed to be recycled. Logan enjoyed cooking, and the results were often something delicious like the lasagna they'd just enjoyed, but the guy was lousy at cleaning up after himself.

Jack turned the faucet to hot and filled the first saucepan with suds, thinking back over the conversation at dinner and the way Maggie rebounded from her chaotic day. When Logan asked why she was on the Cape, she told him the truth. That her sister had been found dead, murdered, and she was here to identify the body. After initially hesitating, she told Logan the rest of the story, about her sister's arrest, her very public humiliation in the media, and the grand jury hearing Cameron was supposed to testify for. Granted, he probably would've told his brother the details eventually, but he was proud of Maggie for getting it out there. Despite the over-whelming feeling that he needed to protect her, she was tough. Stronger than she looked. He hoped Logan appreciated that.

The only thing Maggie didn't come clean about was the ghost at the morgue. Would Logan be able to wrap his head around the fact that Maggie thought she could see her sister's ghost, or that the Medical Examiner claimed he could hear the ghost speak? He loved his brother, but he wasn't sure if he'd believe it. Shit, Jack had been there and watched everything go down and still wasn't sure what to believe. Maybe that's why

Maggie didn't mention the ghost to Logan, wanting to make a good first impression. One that didn't scream "crazy."

"What's really going on between you and that girl?"

Speak of the devil.

Jack kept his focus on the sink, and the sauce pan rinsing under the faucet. "It's police business. She outlined it for you at dinner."

"Bullshit."

Jack glanced over his shoulder, seeing his brother's bulky frame filling the kitchen doorway. "Where is she right now?"

"Asleep on the couch. Out like a light with the cutest little snore." Logan moved to stand next to the sink, his hip cocked against the countertop. "Now spill. Clue me into why she talks about you like you're her own personal superhero."

Something inside Jack swelled, his ego enjoying the stroke. He liked the thought of being Maggie's personal superhero, but he deflected the compliment. "I have no idea what you're talking about."

Logan chuckled, crossing muscled forearms over his chest. "Sure you don't. How long have you two known each other?"

Jack hesitated. "Since about noon."

"Noon? You mean today?" Logan's mouth hung open. "Are you fucking kidding me?"

"No."

"I can't believe this shit. You've known the girl less than half a day and you're head over heels for her."

"Fuck you, Logan." He said it without any heat behind the words, studiously avoiding eye contact. He placed one pan into the drying rack next to the sink and starting to scrub another. "The Medical Examiner sent me out to Worcester to notify her about her sister. I gave her a ride back to his office in Bourne to identify her sister's body. That's all there is to it."

"And what? You thought, *hmm, I like this one so maybe I'll keep her awhile*, and brought her here?" Logan's chuckle reverberated through the kitchen. "Maybe I should quit the construction business and join the force, especially if they let you bring the cute witnesses home at the end of your shift."

"Don't be a jerk. It's not like that." Jack scrubbed a little too vigorously, splashing water onto the counter and floor. "Besides, I wasn't even on the clock today."

"That's right. Today and tomorrow are your days off. Fishing today with Dylan and Ed, and working on the house with me tomorrow. But you didn't go fishing, did you. Sounds like you're going to blow me off like you did the cousins." Logan pushed off from the counter to avoid the fresh puddles of water and suds spreading his way.

"No one's blowing anyone off," Jack growled, pushing away the tantalizing images his brother's words painted in his dirty mind. "But I will need to give her a ride back to Bourne in the morning. She wants to see her sister again."

His heart ached for her, thinking about all the things she'd need to deal with in the wake of her sister's death. He'd determined from their earlier conversation on the drive from Worcester that she had no other family to help her. She was all alone. Maybe he could take a few days off to help her sort through things. He hated to think about her dealing with everything on her own.

Logan interrupted his train of thought. "Yeah? And *then* what's your plan?"

Jack frowned. Had he been talking out loud? "What do you mean?"

"You've known the girl half a day."

Reality smacked him in the face. He barely knew her. She

barely knew him. Why would she want his help with anything? "What's your point?"

"It's obvious you like the girl, bro. What's your plan to see her again after tomorrow?"

The question brought him up short. Because as much as he might want to see more of Maggie, he had no idea what she wanted. How could he make any plans without talking to her first? "I don't really have one."

"Well, you should make one. I've never seen you look at anyone like you look at her. Not even whats-her-face, that ice queen you dated in college."

"You mean Kristie?"

Logan snorted. "Whatever. I mean, who up and leaves a guy when there's a family crisis? When you love someone, you stick around for both the good and the bad. *Especially* for the bad."

"That's not how it went down," Jack argued, his back stiffening. "Our breakup had nothing to do with dad's accident. It was my fault…"

"Bullshit." Logan's eyes flashed with anger. "There is nothing wrong with you, except that you're a terminally good person. I know you thought you loved Kristie, but what'd she ever do for you? You were always there when she needed you, always working your schedule around hers. Christ, we only ever saw you guys in summer when she wanted to spend time on the beach. Not a single holiday or family event in the three years you dated her."

"That can't be right…"

"Fuck that. You know I'm right. I'm sorry, bro, but she used you. And when the going got tough, she left. It's the truth. But for some insane reason you think the breakup was your fault."

"If I hadn't dropped out of school…"

"Mom needed you. I was ready to come home too except

you made me stay in school to keep my scholarship. You're so busy carrying everyone else's burdens that you forget to take care of yourself."

Jack's back teeth began to ache and he realized he'd been clenching his jaw since the start of this conversation. He exhaled, making an effort to relax. "I've been out on dates."

"Tourists. One night stands. When was your last date with a local girl?"

Jack had to think about that for a moment. "Memorial Day weekend. Ed and Dylan's bonfire, remember? I brought Paige Wheeler."

"And her son, who roasted marshmallows and played with our niece. I remember." Logan shook his head in disgust. "You're friends with Paige, and not the friends-with-benefits kind. It's not like you have feelings for her."

No. That would be too weird, Jack thought, considering he was the only one who knew the identity of Paige's baby-daddy. With the added bonus that it was one of his cousins, a fact he promised Paige he'd keep to himself. As much as he might want to beat some sense into his worthless, clueless cousin, she'd sworn him to secrecy years ago, something that went against every grain of his black-and-white sense of fairness. Her kid deserved better. He deserved to know his dad.

He tuned back in to hear the end of his brother's rant. "... and that's why I think you should go for it with Maggie," Logan finished, giving him a crooked smile.

Jack felt an odd combination of relief and annoyance, his jaw tensing again. Relieved that Logan wasn't interested in Maggie for himself, and annoyed that he thought Jack's love life was any of his goddamn business. "I don't think it's up to you to decide."

"No?" Logan challenged, a smirk on his face.

Another voice answered. "No."

The brothers whipped around to find a disgruntled Maggie standing in the kitchen doorway, arms crossed over her chest and green eyes staring daggers at them both.

Oh fuck.

18

Maggie glared at the MacDonald brothers, willing her heart to slow from its gallop to more of a trot. What business did they have arguing over her, as if she were some carnival prize to be won? And who the hell was Paige Wheeler?

And why did Maggie care who Jack dated anyway? He wasn't hers to claim.

Just like she wasn't theirs to argue over.

Moments before, she woke from disturbing dreams to find herself alone on a strange couch in a dark, unfamiliar room with a Bruce Willis action movie that she couldn't name playing on the television. She huddled under the blanket, her heart racing, until the events of the last day filtered back into her conscious mind.

The break-in.

The shooting.

Her sister's murder.

Her sister's *ghost.*

Creepy Carl.

Jack MacDonald.

Meeting Jack was the highlight of a rather dark twenty-four hours. Their near kiss on the floor of her apartment after the shooting kept circling through her brain. There was no way to ignore the fact that Jack made her feel safe. More importantly, he made her feel like she meant something. Like she was more than just a mini-me of her sister. It'd been a long time since she let someone close enough to care, and here she was dropping her guard with a guy she barely knew. Curled up on the most comfortable leather couch she'd ever sat on, let alone fallen asleep on. Wishing with every fiber of her being that he was here lying next to her.

The timing was terrible. Her sister was dead, the killer on the loose. And all she could think about was wanting Jack's muscled arms wrapped around her, holding her tight, lending his strength. Telling her things would be okay. She huffed out a mirthless laugh. Maybe all she wanted was a little bit of comfort and Jack was convenient.

Although his touch felt anything but convenient. The way he looked at her, his eyes hot and intense. Even after everything at the morgue tonight with the ghost, he still treated her with the same kindness and respect. He could've dropped her off at any one of the motels or guest houses they'd passed along the way, but he didn't. Instead, he offered her a warm meal and a place to crash for the night so she wouldn't have to be alone.

Raised voices floated in from another room. Sitting up on the couch, she pushed off the throw blanket someone tucked around her body, stretching her arms overhead. She berated herself for eavesdropping even as she strained to listen.

"It's obvious you like the girl, bro. What's your plan to see her again after tomorrow?"

"I don't really have one."

There was no mistaking Jack's graveled voice. Or the disinterest in the tone of his response, which washed over her like a bucket of ice water. *I don't really have one.* Meaning he'd give her a ride back to the morgue in the morning and be done with her. One more obligation in the line of duty. Obviously, she'd been placing unwarranted importance on their interactions. Reading too much into those hot looks and gentle touches. Without his uniform, she kept forgetting this was just a job for him. When he showed up on her doorstep in his flannel shirt and jeans, she thought he looked like a hot, sexy cowboy. But in that Bruins hoodie? He looked deliciously rumpled and relaxed, a guy she could see herself kicking back and hanging out with every weekend.

Except he had no plans for anything like that. No plans to ever see her again.

Fine. Just fine. She didn't need any more help from the infuriatingly sexy cop. *Fucking hell,* she felt whiplashed from the rollercoaster of her own thoughts and emotions. Of course he didn't have a plan – why would he? In the few hours he'd known her, he'd been held at gunpoint, shot, drenched in tears, and faced with a ghost he couldn't see or hear. Why would he trust anything that came out of Maggie's mouth?

Fueled by anger, and a healthy dose of embarrassment at her own naiveté, she rose from the couch ready to confront Jack and his brother. Standing in the doorway to the kitchen, seeing Jack up to his elbows in suds, sleeves of the hoodie pushed up over his elbows and still damp, her anger wavered. He was so adorable… but then Logan mentioned another woman's name – a woman with a kid – before citing a laundry list of reasons Jack needed to get back on "the proverbial horse."

Proverbial horse? Really? Now I'm a farm animal for the sexy cowboy to ride. Logan's words riled her to no end, but a small piece of her brain latched onto the idea of riding Jack, spearing an arrow of heat and need straight through her.

"…and that's why I think you should go for it with Maggie." Logan finished his ranting diatribe with a crooked smile that would've looked cute if she wasn't as pissed at him.

Jack was shaking his head in disagreement with his brother. "I don't think any of this is up to you to decide."

"No?" Logan's crooked smile turned into a full-on smirk. Maggie felt like slapping it off his face but contented herself by interrupting the conversation.

"No."

The brothers whipped around to find a disgruntled Maggie standing in the kitchen doorway. She crossed her arms over her chest and tried her best to send lazer beams at them with her glare. Not that she'd ever had that particular superpower in the past, but if ever there was a good time to develop a new skill this would be it.

The startled look on Logan's face morphed back into his lazy grin. "Oh hey, Mags. I thought you were asleep on the couch."

"I was, until you knuckleheads woke me with your argument. You MacDonald boys are too much. For the record, neither of you idiots gets a say in…" The sound of a distinctive ringtone made her freeze mid-sentence. Her eyes darted around the kitchen, looking for her bag as Sister Sledge serenaded them with the chorus from *We Are Family*. "That's my sister's ringtone."

Jack grabbed a dishcloth, quickly swiping the suds off his hands. "We left your stuff by the door when we came in." She followed him through the dining room to the entry hall, quickly digging her phone from the bottom of her purse. She stared for a moment at her sister's avatar on the screen, elated and nostalgic and bewildered all at the same time. *Cameron?*

It couldn't be Cameron calling. She'd seen her sister's body in the morgue. Moreover, she'd seen *her sister's ghost* in the morgue. Ghosts don't use cell phones to make contact. Who else would have access to Cameron's cell phone? *Whoever killed her might still have her phone....*

"You gonna answer that?"

Logan's question jarred her from her immobile state. Swiping her finger a second too late, the call automatically switched over to voicemail. "Damn it," she seethed. She looked up to find Jack staring at her with concern. "Do you think they'll leave a message?"

She hated the needy tone of her voice. Hated that she was looking to him to be the voice of reason and compassion when minutes ago he basically told his brother she was nothing more than a job. But she had no one else to turn to. She needed his strength right now.

Jack voice was steady and soft. "Either it's Dan leaving you a message to explain why he shot at us, or..."

"...Or it's the assholes that killed her," she finished. She took a deep breath, her eyes still locked with Jack's. "Either way, they must realize I know Cameron is dead. Why use her phone to call me?"

Jack's mouth dipped into a frown. "Maggie, didn't you tell me that Dan answered your call about the break-in?"

"Yeah?"

He took a step closer, his heat surrounding her. "According to Dr. Miller, your sister was already dead by then."

The implications of his words were clear, but Maggie couldn't go there. She knew Dan. She trusted the guy. He couldn't be the one who hurt her sister. There had to be another explanation.

The phone dinged with an alert that the caller left a message. She automatically started to type in her password but Jack put his large hand on top of hers, stopping her.

"Let's think this through first," he said, his eyes catching hers and holding them captive.

"What? Why?"

"Well…" He pulled his bottom lip in between his teeth and stared off over her shoulder for a moment. "Someone could be trying to trace your whereabouts. Trying to find you." The heat and concern in his eyes was unmistakable. Maggie swallowed the lump forming in her throat, not knowing how to respond.

Logan did it for her. "Why would someone use her sister's phone to try and track her? How would they even do that?"

"There are tons of apps out there that can track down cellphones, especially using a phone on the same plan. The phone has to be turned on and connected to wifi or the web, and the GPS locater does the rest. I'm assuming you and Cameron are on a family plan?"

Maggie nodded, even as Logan was shaking his head. "Why would her sister put a kid tracker on her? She's a grown-ass woman."

"The app comes packaged with the family plan," Jack told his brother. "Maggie, when was the last time you called Cameron?"

"After the break-in, late Saturday. No it would've been early Sunday by then, after the police showed up."

Logan interjected again. "You mean today? This morning?"

Her eyes remained locked with Jack's. "Yeah, today. And Dan answered the phone instead of Cameron, telling me she'd gone back to the hotel to rest. The doctor said Cameron died sometime between Friday night and Saturday morning."

"Yes, he did."

"Dan lied to me on the phone. And he lied to me when he showed up at my apartment this morning. My sister didn't send him to check on me. She was already dead. And he knew it."

"And he still has her phone," Jack added.

"Can anyone track me through a phone message? Is there harm in listening?"

Jack hesitated. "Family finder apps like those don't generally work if the phone is off, or it hasn't been used recently, or it's not connected to the internet. Is your wifi on?" She shook her head. "Unless Dan is working with the police or the phone company, we should be okay, but you should probably turn your phone off as soon as you're done."

After dialing into voicemail and entering her code, Maggie hit the speaker button. Her heart clenched as Dan's voice filled the room. *"Maggie, listen, I'm sorry about what happened earlier but I can explain. I stopped by your diner but they said you went out of town to deal with a death in the family. It's not just me who wants that notebook, Maggie. We need it before the trial. Please call me back."* Click.

Maggie let out a frustrated growl. "I don't have the notebook. Maggie told me she was giving it to the woman from the D.A.'s office. They should already have a copy."

Jack cocked his head to the side, his blue eyes assessing. "You said you visited your sister last weekend in Boston. Did she give you anything?"

"Not her little black book." Maggie waved her hands in the air, moving away from all the intensity coming off Jack in waves. "Hello? Don't you think I'd know if she gave me something that important?"

"Not necessarily." Jack stepped closer again, invading her

space and filling her senses. "She tried to keep you sheltered from her business, right? And from the trial?"

Maggie reluctantly agreed. "Yeah, Dan even said she told him not to discuss things with me." She remembered the crazed look in Dan's eye when he pointed the gun at her, unable to hold back the resulting shiver.

Warm hands slid along her upper arms, dispelling the sudden chill, before sliding around her waist to hold her tight. She tried to focus on better memories. "Cameron and I spent the day in Back Bay. We window shopped on Newbury Street, got our nails done, and watched chick flicks at the house. It was all so normal. We shared a laugh when I told her my roommates didn't understand the appeal of Tom Hardy. She insisted I bring a few of the DVDs back to Worcester. Actually, I'd forgotten about that. They're probably still in my overnight bag."

Jack's eyes darted to the paisley duffle next to the front door. "This same overnight bag? Can you show me?"

Kneeling, she shoved her hand down into the deep outer pocket, pulling out two DVD cases and holding them for Jack to see. "*This Means War,* which we watched Saturday night, and *Venom.* Well, I mean, *Venom* isn't really a chick flick, but Tom Hardy is still too hot for his own good. And Tasha loves super-hero movies so I thought it might be a good introduction. Everyone loves a superhero, right?"

Jack took the DVDs from her, staring at the covers for half a beat before opening the first. Instead of a familiar silver disc, inside the case sat a slim USB flash drive. Pulling the second case open, she saw another flash drive.

"I don't understand…" Maggie removed the bit of clear tape holding each one in place. "Dan said he was searching for an actual notebook. I caught him going through all the books in my room."

"I wonder if these are two copies of the same information, or if there's enough content to split onto separate drives."

Logan cleared his throat and held out a large calloused palm. "There's only one way to find out. Give them to me and we'll check." He caught Maggie's look of surprise and his lips quirked up. "What? You don't think a big guy like me can be computer savvy?"

"He graduated top of his class at Wentworth," Jack explained, a hint of pride in his voice. "You can't design buildings these days without a 3D computer program and mad math skills. My little brother is talented, even if he did get into college on a hockey scholarship."

"Hey now, no need to be hating on the fact I'm the best skater in the family," Logan said, his grin widening. "Better with computers too. Now let's plug-n-play those USB drives."

It turned out the drives held different content. The first one they opened held the content Dan described, a virtual "little black book" but so much more. A large excel file contained dates, names, partners and preferences, as well as columns of basic facts about each man, including phone numbers, job titles, home addresses, marital status… detailed information about each person who availed themselves of the Beacon Hill Beautiful "special" services. A comment column at the end included personal, highly embarrassing details. Tab labels stated the year, with one tab for each year, going back to the 90's.

After copying the information to his hard drive, Logan plugged the second drive into his computer. "Let's see if this is the backup copy." Instead of an excel spreadsheet, a menu of AVI files popped up.

Jack and Maggie stood behind Logan at the desk in the corner of the living room, each perched over one of his broad shoulders. Maggie stared at the screen. "What's an AVI extension mean? Photographs?"

Logan grunted, scrolling down the list of alphabetical names. "Video files. But it looks like they're password encrypted." He tried to click on one and a dialogue box popped up asking for a code to continue.

"I'm not sure we need to watch any videos right now," Maggie said, suppressing a shudder. "Judging by the other file, I'm guessing they're sex tapes, right? Content suitable for blackmail?"

"Most likely," Jack agreed, stroking his chin. "The first one definitely looks like the file the D.A. needs for the grand jury hearings. The video files though... I wonder if anyone knew Cameron had a copy of those. You said Dan was looking for a book, right? If he knew there were videos, he would be looking for a drive, or a disc."

Maggie frowned. "Cameron said she gave her book to the Assistant D.A. Shouldn't the lawyers have all this information, if not the videos?"

"The A.D.A. was found shot in her condo, remember? We have to assume someone took the originals when they killed her." Jack pulled Maggie to him and wrapped his arms around her slight frame.

Logan was still scrolling through the menu of AVI files. "Hey, I recognize a bunch of these names. The mayor of Boston, a bunch of state senators, the state secretary, the state treasurer... looks like everyone in Massachusetts leadership except Governor Plunkett himself."

A wistful smile passed across Maggie's face. "My dad was friends with the governor, back when he first ran for state senate. We belonged to the same country club as his family. To think that now he's planning to run for president."

"There's also a few names I recognize from national politics, although, it's just a last name. Technically these could be anyone. Without watching the videos, we don't know who they are." Logan had grabbed pen and paper and was scribbling down a list of the file names. He looked up at Jack. "What have you gotten yourself into?"

19

Jack met his brother's intense stare, something passing between them. Whatever was going on was definitely dangerous, with Maggie in the middle of it all because of these files. Blackmail, scandal and political corruption on a state and maybe even national level... it seemed overwhelming to contemplate in the middle of the night. Tuesday they could take the files to Bourne and give them to the officials from the D.A.'s office. Except...

"Lo, is the District Attorney for Boston anywhere on those lists? Check for his top aides, too. The videos, or the other one, the client list? You're looking for the names Lacey, Esposito and Salazar. Those were the guys mentioned in that article about A.D.A. Kazinski's murder."

His brother made quick work of checking through names of the videos. "Nope, none of those names are here. Let me check the excel file." He popped out one thumb drive and inserted the other. "No, not here either. You plan to drive the files up to Boston?"

Jack shook his head. "Someone from the D.A. should be in Bourne at the coroner's office Tuesday morning."

"But you're taking me back to that place tomorrow, right?" Maggie gripped his arm as she spoke. "I need to see my sister."

Logan's eyes ping-ponging between the two of them, obviously not understanding her need to view the dead body a second time. Jack wasn't sure how to explain the strange situation to Logan, and wasn't sure whether Maggie would want him to. Claiming the ability to see ghosts – or in Dr. Miller's case, hear them – was unusual enough without the added twist of the murder victim being the only one who could explain Maggie's current, and dangerous, situation.

"I'll take you to see Dr. Miller in the morning, and finish all the paperwork we didn't get to tonight," he assured her, hoping his explanation would appease Logan's curiosity. "I have the day off from work, and can give you a ride back to Worcester as well."

Maggie frowned. "I think I should stick around the Cape to talk with the lawyers from the District Attorney's office on Tuesday morning. Maybe I could even go with them back to Boston, since I'll need to make funeral arrangements up there and... oh shit, I'm sorry! I'm totally imposing on you guys! You had plans to work on the house tomorrow."

"No, no," Jack reassured her, laying his hand over the one that still gripped his arm. "That's not it at all. I thought you'd want to go home as soon as possible. Be with your friends. But if you're good with staying here, please stay. I'll even drive you up to Boston when you're ready. I'd feel a whole lot better knowing you're safe."

Those deep forests of green grew hazy, as if puzzled by his declaration. "Why? I mean, you barely know me."

He felt his face heating with embarrassment, knowing his

little brother bore witness to this scene. What could he tell her that wouldn't sound either completely sappy, or like he was trying to take advantage of her? Before he could answer, Logan let out a loud laugh and elbowed him in the ribs.

"Our Jack here is a real trooper, in every sense of the word. Overdeveloped sense of duty, like the true blue hero he is. He's not going to let you out of his sight until he's sure you're safe."

The light in her eyes dimmed a bit at Logan's words. "Oh. Right. I keep forgetting you're actually a State Trooper."

Jack swallowed hard, not sure how to respond or what she wanted him to say. He *was* a trooper. His job was to protect and serve. But that wasn't the reason he wanted to keep Maggie safe. At least, not the whole reason. He'd only known her half a day, and yet it felt like he'd known her longer. Much longer. "Maggie…"

Logan stepped in, clapping a hand on each of their shoulders. "It's getting late and Mags must be exhausted. Why don't I show her to the guest room while you finish up in the kitchen, Jack? Tomorrow will be soon enough to figure things out." Not waiting for a reply, Logan led Maggie from the room, grabbing her overnight bag on his way.

Jack watched them go, a green monster flaring within when his brother wrapped an arm around Maggie's shoulders. Which was ridiculous, since it wasn't that long ago that Logan stood in the kitchen telling him to "go for it" with Maggie. God help him, he wanted nothing more than to wrap his arms around her and kiss her… but the timing couldn't be worse.

Jack stamped out the flames of jealousy burning his gut. He had no claims to the woman. So why did she feel like his to protect? She wasn't. This was a case, nothing more. He'd been first on the scene to discover Cameron Nelson's body, and he'd also happened to be on the scene to protect Maggie from the guy who probably killed her sister. He was simply doing his job.

Except "simple" went out the window when Maggie and the coroner claimed a ghost was involved. Jack didn't believe in the existence of ghosts. The fact that Maggie claimed to see her sister at the morgue should be a huge red flag warning him to steer clear.

He scrubbed a hand through his hair, blowing out the breath he'd been holding. He'd see this case through the rest of the weekend. He'd take her back to fill out the paperwork in the morning, and figure out something to keep her entertained until the D.A.'s office came to claim the body Tuesday morning. At that point, the dead body, the thumb drives full of evidence, and the girl who saw ghosts would all be someone else's problem.

So why did that make his gut churn with anxiety?

2 0

Monday, October 14, 4:00 a.m.
23 Crosswind Farm Road, Chatham

Maggie startled awake from disturbing dreams, unable to place her surroundings. She'd fallen asleep with the light on, and the pale blue walls with bright white trim let her know she wasn't in her own bedroom. The empty spot next to her also let her know she hadn't made a grave error in judgement, ending up in some frat boy's bed.

Yesterday's events filtered back through her brain like a slow-motion horror movie, assailing her emotions yet again. She remembered with absolute clarity where she was. And why.

Cameron is dead.

Fresh tears wet her cheeks. She would've thought she'd run out of tears by now, but apparently not. She turned her face into the pillow to muffle any noise, not wanting to wake Logan or Jack in the middle of the night. Especially not Jack. He'd already put up with so much from her, above and beyond what duty called for.

While it hurt to realize she was nothing more than a case for him, she was still glad to have him by her side. It was all too overwhelming to deal with on her own. Blackmail... Shooting... Murder... these weren't things Maggie ever expected to come face to face with in her lifetime.

Not to mention her sister's ghost. Which seemed to be the only part Jack struggled with.

Wiping the moisture from her cheeks, she rose from the bed. She needed something to drink, but at four in the morning, water would have to suffice. In the darkened kitchen, moonlight streamed in the window outlining a dark silhouette by the sink. Her breath caught in her throat. "Cameron?" she whispered.

The low, very male chuckle sent a shiver dancing along her skin. "No ghosts, Maggie. It's just me." The shadow moved a step closer, his face and torso illuminated by the moonlight. Jack stood before her wearing nothing but a pair of dark sweatpants slung low on his hips. Her gaze caught for a long moment on his bandaged shoulder, the white gauze almost glowing in the slightly blue light, before her eyes drifted down across the wide expanse of muscled chest to the well-defined V at his waist. The man was chiseled to perfection, like a fantasy come to life.

"Jack... What are you doing awake so early?" She crossed her arms over pebbled nipples, all too aware of the flimsy cotton of her nightshirt and the fact she wasn't wearing a bra. She tried to focus on the gunshot wound, evidenced by the white bandage, and the fact that she was nothing but a job to him. No good would come from wanting him the way she did right this moment. The sheer intensity of her need took her breath away.

"Couldn't sleep. You?" He leaned against the counter, his face fading back into the shadows, his arms crossing to mimic her stance. Her eyes adjusted to the darkness, focused on the bulging biceps, at the obvious strength on display. She finally tore her eyes away from his arms, but his knowing smirk said he'd noticed the lingering look.

She shrugged, trying to calm her racing heart. "Nightmares woke me."

The smirk disappeared, replaced with concern. "Maggie, I'm so sorry about your sister. Now that we discovered the information she hid with you, we can start finding answers."

She swallowed hard and nodded in agreement. "I've got a lot of questions to ask her when we go back to see Dr. Miller."

Jack stood silent, his expression carefully blank.

"I can tell you still don't believe in ghosts." For some reason, his skepticism bothered her.

"I'm not sure what I believe," he answered carefully. "And there's obviously something going on that I can't explain. I'd like to keep an open mind about it all for the moment, if that's okay."

She nodded even as her hackles rose. "Better than calling me crazy."

Those blue eyes filled with pain. "I would never call you crazy, Maggie. Just because we can't explain what's going on doesn't mean it's not happening. "

His words went a long way toward soothing her ruffled feathers. "I know it's hard to understand, especially if you can't see or hear her. But my sister was there, standing right next to the doctor, wearing one of her designer dresses and looking as perfect as always."

He held up both hands. "I'm on your side, Maggie. It's not the idea of ghosts keeping me awake, but I am worried about the thumb drives your sister hid with you. I want to keep you safe, and I don't know the best way to do that."

"Why? Why do you feel this need to *keep me safe*? What makes it your responsibility, Jack? Because it's your job?" She drew a deep breath and waited, holding in that breath.

He looked away, unable to meet her intense gaze. "I just do, okay?"

Maggie's shoulders sagged. Not the answer she'd hoped for. Not much of an answer at all, really. "I'm not trying to pick a fight, Jack. I actually came in here looking for water." She reached behind him to grab a glass out of the drying rack. She pushed him to the side with her hip and turned on the faucet. A sharp intake of breath had her glancing up into his face.

"Maggie..." The look in his eyes was an odd mix of longing and resignation.

She licked her lips and made a decision. She'd spent too much time over the last twelve hours thinking about kissing this guy, and after tomorrow she might never see him again. Especially since she was just another *job* to him. Pressing one hand against his bare chest, the heat of his skin nearly seared her fingers. She went up on her toes, whispering a soft kiss across his lips. "Thank you for keeping me safe, Officer MacDonald."

His chest rumbled under her hand and she felt the vibration all the way to her core. She sunk her teeth into her bottom lip, the pinch a painful reminder that anything she felt was one-sided. His eyes zeroed in on her mouth. When he spoke, his voice sounded more like a growl. "Maggie..."

"What?"

He pushed off from the counter, crowding her backward,

her hand slipping down from his chest. The heat from his body surrounded her, the smell of him invading her senses. She bumped against the counter behind her. His large hands came to rest on her hips, caging her in.

"I don't know how to explain it since we only met yesterday. But Maggie, you are so much more to me than just a job. You make me want things…" His eyes held hers as he spoke, searching for something, maybe some sign that she was on the same page. Because he was certainly making her *want things*, as he so inelegantly stated.

"What sort of things do you want?" Maggie barely recognized her own breathy voice.

"I need… I need to touch you." His whispered words seemed loud in her ears, resonating through her body. She saw it in his eyes, the moment his decision was made. With another low growl, his mouth crashed against hers, his kiss anything but soft. His large hands gripped her hips, holding her in place as he ravaged her mouth, his tongue begging her to open for him and she did. Every nerve ending in her body felt electrified, every part of her body aching for his touch. Her hands slid up his solid chest, snaking around his neck to pull him closer, losing herself in his kiss. All sense of place and time obliterated until everything in the universe came down to her and him, and this one moment in the dark.

Until the phone on the counter behind her rang, the harsh sound crashing through them both, Jack springing away as if she were an open flame. The phone rang again as they stood staring at each other, panting, trying to catch their breath. The overhead light suddenly flicked on, shining bright, unflinching light onto the situation.

Logan stopped short in the doorway, looking between Jack and Maggie as the harsh ringing filled the kitchen a third time.

Maggie noted the faded Wentworth t-shirt over plaid boxers, Logan's bedhead making it obvious he'd been fast asleep moments before. "Um, Jack? Can you answer the phone?"

Maggie hurried to step out of the way, unable to meet anyone's eyes. She tuned out both brothers, the only sound in her ears the pounding of her blood, embarrassed by her own brazen behavior. What was she thinking, kissing Jack like she had a right to? Acting as if her visit to Cape Cod was some sort of vacation getaway rather than the dangerous situation her sister's murder left her in. A glance at the wall clock surprised her, showing it was well after five. The moon sat low on the horizon, the sky a lighter shade of darkness than before.

Jack cleared his throat and spoke her name. She face him, seeing Logan standing next to his brother wearing a look of concern. "That was Myrna Miller. Sam never came home last night.

21

---

*J*ack watched her take in his statement. The smell of her still filled his senses, the vanilla and lavender mix that drove him wild. He wanted to hug her close and keep her safe... hell, he wanted more than anything to continue that kiss the phone call interrupted. To see where it might lead. To throw her over his shoulder and hide away in his bedroom until all of this was over. But he couldn't. Not now. Not with his brother standing right next to him in his under-wear with a worried look on his face. Not with another life potentially at risk.

"What does that mean? Why did the doctor's wife call you?"

He scrubbed a hand through his hair. "Sam called her last night to let her know he'd be late for dinner. That he was with you and me at the morgue and didn't know how late he'd be there. He wasn't home when she went to bed at ten."

She stared at him and he felt like he could see the wheels turning in her head as she remembered the prior evening.

"But... but we got here around eight. Shouldn't he have left then too?"

Jack nodded. "He said he was going to see if he could find any more information before he locked up and went home."

"But he didn't go home." It was a statement, not a question.

"She just woke up and realized he never did make it to bed and his car wasn't in their driveway. When no one answered at the morgue, she called the local police, who advised her she needed to wait a bit longer before filing a missing person report. She remembered my name and that I lived in Chatham, and looked up my number."

"So what does she want you to do?"

He shrugged. "She wanted to know what time we left him there, or if I knew of a reason he might not have gone home. I wasn't sure what to tell her other than the time we left and that he planned to head home soon after." After he spoke with the ghosts again, or whatever it was he planned to do. Not that Jack believed in ghosts. But like he told Maggie before, there seemed to be a lot going on that he couldn't rationally explain.

"What do we do now? He knew we planned to drive back up there this morning to talk with him." Jack wondered if the anxiety lacing her voice was for the missing doctor, or the missed opportunity to "talk" with her dead sister. "Could he have fallen asleep at his desk? Or do you think it's something... sinister?"

Up until that point, Jack wasn't completely sure Maggie appreciated the danger of her situation. The way she whispered the word sinister sent a chill up his spine and left no doubt that she understood. If the doctor hadn't sent Jack to Worcester yesterday, there was a good chance she'd be in a situation similar to the one Cameron had been in mere days before.

"I don't know. That's why I'm going to Bourne to check on him."

"I'm coming with you. Give me a sec to throw on some clothes." Maggie raced out of the kitchen before he could respond, leaving Jack and Logan staring after her.

Logan broke the silence. "Is it a good idea to let her tag along?"

Jack quirked an eyebrow at his brother. "Does it look like she's giving me a choice?"

Logan blew out a long breath. "Need me to come along and ride shotgun, so to speak?"

"Shit. The Worcester cops kept my gun." He shouldn't walk into an unknown situation without a sidearm.

"That nails it then. I'm coming along and literally bringing my hunting rifle." Logan lumbered out into the hallway. Jack followed, arguing.

"You could let me borrow the rifle and go back to bed, Lo. You don't need to do this on your day off."

Logan turned and faced him, hands on hips. "Jack, what kind of brother would I be if I let you go face potential danger on your own and unarmed? I've got your back."

Jack shook his head, laughing. "You know I work in law enforcement, right? I face potential danger every fucking day on the job."

Logan stopped at his bedroom door. "Then let me come protect Mags." When Jack started to protest, Logan held up a hand to silence him. "Not stepping on your toes there either, dude. I'm not an idiot. But if she rides along, she's gonna distract you. Let me help."

He thought on his brother's words for a moment before giving him a curt nod. "Be ready to go in five. And Logan... thanks."

22

Monday, October 14, 6:30 a.m.
Barnstable County Medical Examiner and Coroner's office, Bourne

$\mathcal{H}$e tried to get her to wait in the truck, to no avail. At least she'd agreed to bring up the rear of their little trio, safely hidden behind his mountain of a brother. They pulled into the parking lot of the coroner's building along with the rising sun, and saw everything looked normal, Sam's sedan still parked in the same spot as yesterday. Maybe Maggie was been right on the money with her "fallen asleep at his desk" theory, but nothing this weekend had been as easy – or normal – as it should be.

Surprised to find the front double doors unlocked, he tried once again to get Maggie to wait in the parking lot but she refused.

"Then remember to stay behind Logan," he told her. He

turned and headed for the stairs, noting that nothing seemed broken or out of place in the lobby. The building was quiet. Too quiet. Then again, it was a federal holiday, so it's not like he expected it to be crowded, especially with dawn barely breaking outside.

The hallway in the basement also stood silent and pristine as Jack inched his way toward the doctor's office at the end of the hallway. The tiny hairs on the back of his neck itched with an anticipation bordering on dread. He'd visited these offices plenty of times over the last few years, but never experienced the ominous feeling he had right this moment. Behind him, the door to the stairwell clanged shut, making him flinch. He scowled back at his brother, who merely shrugged, the hunting rifle hanging loosely by his side. Obviously, Logan wasn't getting the same creepy vibe from the place that he was. Jack blew out a long breath before slowing pushing open the door to Dr. Miller's office and workroom.

It looked like a tornado had whirled through. Papers and files lay strewn across the floor. Filing cabinets overturned. Doc's cabinet of medical tools stood open, metal tools of all shapes and sizes scattered around the room.

He heard Maggie's gasp behind him a split second before he focused on the body tied to the chair by the desk, blood pooling on the floor beneath him. "Doc!" He sprinted across the small space before turning to bark at Logan. "Keep her out in the hall!"

Blood dripped steadily from a gaping cut on his forehead. Jack put a hand against Sam's throat, checking for a pulse. Weak, but still there.

"Is he alive?" Maggie hovered next to him, her hand on Jack's back.

"I asked you to wait in the hall." Jack pulled out his cell to dial 9-1-1, taking a quick inventory of the desk area, looking for a clean cloth to apply pressure to the head wound.

"No, you told your brother to keep me away. Tell me. Is he…dead?"

"Alive," Jack bit out before the emergency operator answered. He identified himself, gave her the location information and requested both an ambulance and a crime scene unit. Hanging up the phone, he turned to Maggie, grabbing her arm and pulling her toward the door. "You're going to contaminate the scene. Logan, take her back to the truck."

She yanked out of his grasp. "Stop bossing me around. I have every right…" Her words stopped short as she focused on something behind Jack. Her eyes widened into saucers. "Cameron? What is it?"

Jack spun, even though logic told him no one was there. The space behind him was empty. He glanced at Logan, noting the deep frown pulling at his brother's mouth. Maybe he should've warned him about the situation, how Maggie thought she could see her sister's ghost.

Too late now.

He took a deep breath. He still didn't quite believe in ghosts, but he had to admit there was a lot going on with this case that he couldn't explain. For now, humoring Maggie was the easiest course of action. "She's here with us now?"

Maggie licked her lips, looking nervous. "Yes, but she's faded, like she was last night at the end. What did Dr. Miller say about recharging? It doesn't look like that worked for her. Cameron slow down. I can't understand what you're trying to tell us."

Logan opened his mouth to ask a question but Jack cut him off. "Lo, go upstairs and wait for the ambulance. I need to find something to stop the bleeding."

"What about…" Logan's eyes cut to Maggie, who was still conversing with the empty spot next to the doctor's desk.

Jack shook his head. "I'll keep an eye on her. And Logan, keep the rifle out of sight unless you want it taken for evidence."

With a brisk nod, Logan disappeared back into the hallway, leaving Jack to deal with things alone. First things first. He spied a pile of white towels stacked on a shelf, miraculously untouched when the rest of the room was in chaos. Grabbing the one off the top, he folded it smaller and pressed it gently to the doctor's head to stem the bleeding. He gave Sam a quick once over, looking for other wounds. Nylon rope wrapped around his torso secured him to the back of the chair, his arms tight against his sides. There was no indication how long he'd been like that or what exactly happened. Was it connected to Cameron's death? Was someone looking for the files she hid?

Did Sam's call to the D.A.'s office put his life at risk? Or did the same people who trashed Maggie's apartment follow them from Worcester to Bourne? The many variables in this equation made Jack's head start to hurt. Or maybe that was from lack of sleep and lack of caffeine.

"Is there anything I can do to help while we wait for the rescue squad?"

Maggie's voice jolted him from his thoughts. He'd almost forgotten she was still in the room. He shook his head without looking her way. "Logan is upstairs to direct them. If you want to prop open that door to the hall, the ambulance should be here any minute."

She nodded and did as he asked. He noticed she seemed subdued and remembered how she'd fainted after her first ghostly interaction. "Hey, you okay?"

Another nod. He saw her eyes glisten with moisture before she turned her head away.

More tears. Fuck. "Maggie, talk to me. What's going on?" Before she could answer, he heard commotion in the hallway. The ambulance arrived with the rescue squad and police.

Maggie's tears would have to wait.

———————

While the EMTs strapped Sam to a gurney, Jack called Myrna to let her know he'd be taken to Falmouth Hospital. The man still hadn't regained consciousness, so they had more questions than answers around what actually happened. The local cops who were first on scene speculated that kids broke in looking for drugs, and that it was Sam's bad luck to be working late. In deference to the victim, they held off on making junkie jokes until after the ambulance crew wheeled Sam out, but then the cops went to town, wondering what kind of crackheads would break into a morgue to look for drugs? The kind who had a death wish, apparently.

Jack wasn't buying it. Not with everything else he knew.

He watched the investigators photograph the scene and dust for prints in between taking swigs from their extra-large Dunkin' to go cups. *At least they left the bags of donuts in the cruiser.* Jack bit his tongue to keep from lashing out. The local cops were just doing their job, and he shouldn't criticize... unless he wanted to involve them in something he didn't quite understand himself. Was this really a random break-in looking for drugs, or was it connected to Cameron Nelson's murder?

When the detective in charge finally dismissed them, Jack drove Logan and Maggie back to Chatham, the silence in the car heavy with unspoken thoughts and questions.

"I'm headed back to Falmouth to sit with Myrna at the hospital," he told Logan when they reached their house. "You two should try to get some sleep."

Maggie hopped back into the truck. "I'm coming with you." The determined look on her face said she wouldn't be dissuaded. Logan pulled the rifle from the backseat, before looking at Jack and quirking one eyebrow.

Jack shook his head. "Nah, you can put that thing away for now. The cops were convinced it was kids looking for drugs. Not connected to the sex tape scandal." Not that Jack completely believed that, but it's not like he could take a hunting rifle into the hospital with him. He wanted to be there when the doc regained consciousness. Needed to know if his injuries were connected, if Dan Koslov was involved.

He tried one more time with Maggie. "Are you sure you won't stay here? You look exhausted."

She leveled him with those sharp green eyes. "Flattery will get you nowhere," she deadpanned. "I'm coming with you."

"Fine. It'll be easier to keep an eye on you if we're together."

Logan shut the door and tapped it twice with his palm. "Stay safe."

2 3

Monday, October 14, 2:00 p.m.
Falmouth Hospital, 100 Ter Heun Drive, Falmouth

*M*aggie hadn't seen the inside of a hospital – any hospital – in too many years to count. Not since she'd broken her arm jumping off a swing in elementary school, and then it had been Mass General in downtown Boston. Her memories of that ginormous hospital swirled with a constant stream of people rushing everywhere. Nurses, doctors, patients, families... so many people, so much noise and confusion. Scary for an eight-year old. This was her first time returning and it didn't seem nearly as formidable as her memories.

Falmouth Hospital seemed smaller by every possible measure. Jack and Maggie were the only two in the third floor waiting room. The only live people, anyway. There was a faded silhouette of a man pacing up and down the opposite side of the small room whom Maggie was doing her best to ignore. Apparently seeing ghosts was her new normal, whether she chose to embrace it or not.

In the time it took Jack and Maggie to drive to Chatham and back again, the trauma unit team stitched Dr. Miller's head wound in the emergency room before sending him for x-rays and full CT scans. His wife now sat with him in the recovery area, waiting for test results, or for Sam to awaken, whichever came first. One of the local cops leaned against the nurses' station, flirting with one of the women on duty and waiting to take a victim statement. Jack had checked in with him when they arrived at the hospital. No change in the doctor's state as yet.

Maggie needed to know if the break-in had anything to do with Cameron's death. She figured it had to, right? The timing was too coincidental to be an anything else, no matter what she overheard the cops at the scene saying about teenagers and drugs.

Cameron's ghost had been there, hovering near the doctor's desk, obviously trying to tell her something important about whatever happened to Sam Miller. If only she could hear rather than merely see her sister's ghost. Speaking of which, another ghost wandered passed the waiting room of the hospital, her face a mask of grief, her mouth open in a mournful wail. *Maybe it was a good thing not to hear them after all.*

She kept her head down, not wanting the ghosts to suspect her ability. What good could she do for anyone if she couldn't understand their words? She couldn't help anyone resolve their issues. She couldn't even understand what Cameron was trying to warn her about.

Because she'd totally been trying to warn her about something.

Maggie glanced over at Jack, who hadn't strung together more than three words at a time since leaving Logan at the house. "Talk to me, Jack. I'm starting to worry about you."

He refused to meet her gaze. "I don't like hospitals." When she didn't respond, he finally relented and filled in the gaps. "My dad was in a car wreck when I was in grad school. He nearly died in this very hospital."

She reached for his hand automatically. "I'm so sorry. I didn't know."

He finally met her eyes. "It's okay. I'm okay, and more importantly, so is my dad. But... the whole thing changed the course of my life."

"How so?"

"It was a hit and run. Drunk driver. Repeat offender. No one held the guy accountable any of the other times he'd been caught, so he still had his license. Still out on the highway able to hurt people."

She put two and two together. "Which is why you joined law enforcement."

"Yup." He blew out a long breath. "First I stayed home and helped Mom with the bed and breakfast while Dad recovered. Then dropped out of law school and went to the police academy."

"What about Logan?"

"He helped out over the summer when he was home on break, but I didn't want him to give up his scholarship or his dreams."

"You gave up yours," Maggie pointed out.

Jack laughed, the smile not reaching his eyes. "Turns out it wasn't really my dream but more my girlfriend at the time. She's the one who wanted to be part of a power couple and make a shit-ton of money. I just wanted to make a difference in the world."

At the mention of his college girlfriend, it felt like the bottom dropped out of Maggie's stomach. She gave herself a mental kick in the ass. Of course he dated. Of course he'd be the kind of committed boyfriend who helped his girlfriend succeed in her dreams. Instead of the kind who sold her out for a chance at a TV pilot.

He seemed to sense her internal struggle. "Kristie is long gone, trust me."

Flustered by his powers of observation and embarrassed to be so transparent, she shook her head. "No, I was thinking more about you wanting to make a difference in the world. Guess that explains the undergrad philosophy degree you mentioned last night."

He shrugged. "Gotta understand the world first in order to exact change."

"You're a complicated man, Jack MacDonald."

One corner of his mouth hitched up. "I guess that depends."

"On what?"

"On whether you like complicated."

A different sort of flutter in her stomach left her a little breathless. Before she could come up with a response, a nurse walked into the waiting area. "Mr. MacDonald?"

Jack stood.

The woman nodded at him. "Mrs. Miller is asking for you. Her husband is conscious but he lost a lot of blood. I can't let you into the recovery room, but she said he has a message for you. If you could follow me, I'll let you speak with her in the hallway." He glanced at Maggie but the nurse shook her head. "Just you, I'm afraid. This is already breaking protocol."

"Go, Jack. I'll be fine waiting here." Maggie tried to give him a reassuring smile, but wasn't sure she pulled it off enough to convince him. He stared at her a minute longer until she made a shooing motion with both hands. "Go on, don't leave Myrna waiting."

Jack nodded once before following the nurse down the hallway. Maggie watched him go until he passed the same female ghost she'd seen earlier. Determined not to engage any of the spirits roaming the hospital, she quickly averted her gaze. Instead she found the local cop staring straight at her. His eyes narrowed. She swallowed the lump in her throat as he pushed off from the counter of the nurses' station and stalked toward her.

"Excuse me," the guy said, his voice neutral, thumbs hooked in his belt. "Don't I know you from somewhere?"

Maggie sighed and nodded. "Were you one of the policemen at the Medical Examiner office in Bourne? I gave my statement about the break-in there earlier."

The cop shook his head. "Nah, that's not it. I mean like on TV or something. Are you someone famous? Your face looks so familiar."

Because I look just like Cameron. Maggie huffed another sigh. "You're probably thinking of my sister. Cameron Nelson?"

The cop's eyes went wide. "The Beacon Hill Madam is your sister? Oh man! That must be why you look so freakin' hot. Some of the stories in the media about that place are wild."

Maggie mumbled something incoherent, hoping he'd move along. No such luck.

He snapped his fingers. "That's it. You were the sister with the boyfriend who told his story on the news! Not that ménage a trois are my thing, but I could be persuaded."

Yet another instance where lazer beam-eyeballs would come in oh-

so-handy. "Listen, buddy, my ex made it all up. He never set foot in the spa, not once."

"Are you sure? He sounded pretty convincing."

"Positive." She gave him her best glare, wishing those super-powers would kick in any second.

The cop shrugged and looked like he might be on the verge of an apology when his eyes narrowed a second time. "Wait, isn't the Madam wanted for questioning right now up in Boston, regarding a murder?" His hand slid back along the belt to the holster and rested on his gun. "Is Cameron Nelson here with you today, ma'am?"

"No she's not here with Cameron, shit-for-brains."

Jack was back, and she welcomed the angry edge in his voice.

She cleared her throat, and gave Jack a grateful look before squaring her shoulders to face the rude cop. "We're here to see Dr. Miller."

The guy ignored her and squared off with Jack, going toe to toe but having to tilt his head because of Jack's height advantage. "Oh yeah? And what's the doc got to do with the Beacon Hill Madam? Is he a customer?"

"He's her coroner, you dumbass. Cameron was murdered earlier this weekend."

"But the news said…"

Jack flashed his credentials as he spoke, each word clipped. "I found the body on the side of Route 6. I'm pretty sure."

The cop's chest deflated as he looked at the shield and the information seemed to click in his head. He shot an unreadable glance at Maggie. "Sorry for your loss," he mumbled.

Jack stepped between the cop and Maggie again, blocking him from her view. "Do your job. Go get a victim statement while Dr. Miller is awake and catch the fuckers who threatened his life." The cop mumbled something more before shuffling down the hallway and out of sight.

"You okay?"

Maggie looked up into those true blue eyes, now filled with concern. She tried to shrug off the interaction. "I'm used to everyone mistaking me for her since we look alike." She paused. "I mean *looked* alike. I try to take it as a compliment, since she's so much more sophisticated and put together than I am."

He sat on the edge of the seat next to her and laid a hand on her knee. His eyes crinkled at the corners, his mouth curving into a gentle smile. "You're perfect the way you are, Maggie Nelson."

She rolled her eyes to stave off the sudden onslaught of tears. "We're not here to talk about me. What was the message Dr. Miller wanted you to have?"

The smile faded. "His attackers were looking for the black book. And you."

"Me?"

He nodded. "Doc told me last night Cameron admitted she broke under torture. They knew you were coming to identify the body. They want those USB sticks."

"What do we do?"

Jack stared back at her for a long moment.

It took her a second to realize her mistake. "I mean, what do *I* do? Me, not we. You don't need to be involved in my mess. You've already done plenty." Despite his warm hand on her knee, they weren't a couple. Not really. And there was no reason for him to dig himself any deeper down into the rabbit hole Maggie had fallen into.

The hand on her knee squeezed her tight, those true blue eyes boring into her like he could see into her very soul. "Maggie, I'm in this with you to the end. I've got your back."

She swallowed hard as his words sunk in, warming her. And then her stomach growled loud enough her roommates probably heard it back in Worcester.

A look of surprise registered on Jack's face. "Have you had anything today but coffee?"

"One of the cops this morning shared his box of donut holes with Logan and me while you were being interviewed." Her stomach rumbled again.

"Right. Let's find you some proper food. Coffee and donuts are cop food, not people food."

"Bite your tongue!" Maggie's admonishment came with a smile instead of censure, as she repeated her line from the day before. "Coffee solves all life's problems in one delightful little cup."

Jack rolled his eyes. "So you keep trying to explain. However, I think we should find some proper lunch. We can come back in an hour or so when Dr. Miller is out of the recovery room to see if he's up to talking more."

"Okay. I noticed a sign for a cafeteria on the first floor."

Pain flashed through his eyes. "I spent too many hours there when my dad was hospitalized after the accident. Do you like fried seafood? There's a place a block from here that's decent." Without waiting for her answer, he took her by the hand and led her to the elevator. As they waited side by side, he surprised her by twining their fingers together instead of letting go.

She looked up at him, and found his eyes focused on her. "What?"

Jack pressed his lips together, obviously trying to decide how to say whatever it was he was holding back.

"Just tell me."

The elevator dinged and the doors slid open. They stepped in and he pressed the button for the ground level before turning to face her. "The other thing Doc said was that your sister saved him. That she caused all the chaos we saw in the office, and scared off the attackers."

Maggie stared at him, unable to formulate a response.

Finally, he looked away, shaking his head. "I know, I know. I'm the one who doesn't believe in ghosts. However, it keeps getting harder to explain everything that's happened and stay true to my philosophical beliefs."

"I know you don't want to believe, Jack, but they're real. Ghosts exist."

He tightened his grip on her hand. "Let's just say I'm still reserving final judgement. I'm more concerned with the real live men who attacked the doctor in his office. They're out there now searching for you."

She nodded. On this point at least, they were in perfect agreement. "I should call my roommates and warn them to be careful."

"Good idea, although the bad guys seem to know you came to the Cape."

"Dan." He'd left that message for her yesterday. He'd spoken to Mike at the diner and knew she left Worcester to deal with a death in the family. Unlike her boss, Dan also knew Cameron was the only family Maggie had in the world.

"I'll call Logan and ask him to go through the computer files again, double check the list of names against the D.A.'s office before we meet with them tomorrow. Maybe check specifically for Koslov's name, too. We don't know who we can trust, or who at the state level is already compromised. Right now, the only thing we've got going for us is they don't know where to find you or the files."

24

Monday, October 14, 6:30 p.m.
On the road back to Chatham

*H*eavy traffic headed off-Cape, but it was smooth sailing down Route 6 headed east to Chatham. He glanced over at Maggie. Her head leaned against the side window, but he could see in the window reflection that her eyes were open, staring at the shadowy trees along the side of the darkened highway. Clouds had rolled in sometime during the afternoon. Instead of the purples and navy blues of twilight, the landscapes were dark and ominous.

Unlike their drives to and from Chatham earlier in the day, the silence in the truck felt comfortable instead of heavy. Since leaving the hospital for lunch they'd talked quite a bit, sharing childhood stories and comparing Boston college experiences.

They bonded over their mutual love of watching Red Sox games from the bleachers, and riding bicycles along the Charles River during warm spring months. They argued over the renaming of the Boston Garden and whether the Bruins had a shot at the Stanley Cup. The compared the best concerts they'd seen at the venue, both agreeing in the end that Roger Waters had used the large open space to its best advantage on his most recent tour. Jack felt like he knew Maggie on a deeper level than was warranted after only two days. Knew her, liked her, and wanted to know even more.

He pulled off exit 11 for Chatham. "Almost home," he told her. "We should be back to the house in fifteen minutes."

"Cape Cod is nothing like I imagined it," she said, her forehead still pressed to the glass.

"What do you mean?" He slowed to a stop for a red light, turning to look at Maggie.

"Do you realize I've been on Cape Cod more than twenty four hours now, and have yet to see the ocean or walk on a beach?" She faced him. "Not like I'm here for a vacation or anything, but I pictured a different Cape Cod in my head. Cute little tourist shops along a quaint Main Street, imposing lighthouses towering over white sand beaches with waving seagrass..." her voice trailed off as she shrugged. "You know, like in the movies."

Jack couldn't help the smile quirking his lips. "Yeah, we actually have all that. Tourist shops, lighthouses, beaches, the whole nine yards. We also have brick office buildings and hospitals like anywhere else, obviously."

She looked embarrassed and he took one hand off the steering wheel to pat her leg. "How about we drive the long way home, and I show you Chatham's main street, with all those cute touristy shops and restaurants. We could even stop and have a drink at my cousin's new bar, or dinner out somewhere. It's a seasonal community, so not every place is open this time of year, but there's still plenty to choose from."

Maggie let out a small laugh. "Jasmine suggested I make you buy me a lobster dinner."

"If that's what you're in the mood for," Jack agreed. He ran down the list of restaurants open this time of year in his head. The Inn was the only one he could think of that might be serving a full lobster dinner in the middle of October. Except they were closed on Mondays.

"No need for lobster. I'm not really hungry since we had seafood for lunch a few hours ago."

"Would you like to stop and get a drink at my cousin's place then? He and his wife opened one of those themed martini bars on Main Street this fall. They're trying to work out all the kinks before next summer's rush of tourists."

"One of the famous cousins you were telling me about?"

Jack shook his head. "No, Brian's younger brother is the famous musician. But Brian certainly played a part in a bunch of those stories I told you earlier, about all the trouble us MacDonald boys used to get into as kids."

She leaned her head back against the window, staring out into the growing darkness. "If it's all the same to you, I don't think I'm up to meeting new people right now."

Of course she's not up for going out to a bar, you idiot. Jack gave himself a mental kick in the ass. After the events of the last few days, he was surprised Maggie was holding it together as well as she was. "I can still drive the long way home. Downtown Chatham is pretty at night, with all the stores lit up and decorated for fall." Without waiting for her to agree, he made the turn that would take them in the right direction and soon enough they were driving down Main Street. Scarecrows and pumpkins featured heavily in every display, more harvest themed than Halloween.

"You were right," Maggie admitted. "This is cute. Kinda reminds me of Woodstock or Stowe, up in Vermont."

"I've only been to Burlington, back in college," Jack admitted. "You know, for hockey games at UVM."

"Really? You're totally missing out. We should totally go to Woodstock. I mean, *you*. You should totally take a trip north." Her hands fumbled in her lap, fingers twisting together as if embarrassed to suggest he might want to road trip with her. He rested one hand on top of hers to still the nervous movements.

"I'd love to visit Woodstock with you." He slowed to a stop to let a group of people cross the road and glanced over at her. Their eyes locked for a moment and in that split second he swore he glimpsed the future, with Maggie by his side holding his hand. Everything inside him settled as he lost himself in her emerald eyes.

Until the car behind them honked, bringing him back to reality.

He cleared his throat and removed his hand from atop hers, gesturing at the various shops. "Harvest festival is next weekend, in between Columbus Day weekend and Halloween. Sidewalk sales at all the shops, hot cider and a Bavarian style "oompah" group at the bandstand in the park. Carnival games for the kids and a pumpkin lighting on Saturday night. All the small town silliness you can imagine."

"Sounds pretty great." Her voice was barely a whisper as they passed the lighted shop windows. Once they finally left the downtown area, she turned her body to face him. "You grew up with lots of small town traditions, here, huh?"

He nodded. "Everyone thinks of Chatham in summer, when

it's a busy tourist town. We're actually just a little fishing town most of the year. Where people know their neighbors and look out for one another, you know?"

She was silent for a moment before shaking her head. "I grew up in Boston, so no, I don't really know what small town life is like. It sounds nice."

The wistful tone in her voice make his chest tight. He nodded his agreement, unable to get any words out.

Her eyes got a faraway look to them. "When we were growing up, my parents used to take us up to Vermont this time of year, to Manchester or Woodstock or Stowe... you know, to see the foliage and visit art galleries and antique shops and stuff. When I was little that was my dream, to leave the big city and live in a place like that. Maybe that's why I want to be an artist."

He nodded. "Sounds like a good goal to have."

She huffed out a laugh. "Yeah, right. Not compared to your *whole make the world a better place*. I just want to paint pretty pictures and know my neighbors by name."

"Don't do that."

"Do what?"

"Put yourself down like that. You're a good person, Maggie. You deserve to be happy."

She made a noncommittal noise. He glanced over at her, and was about to argue the point when her stomached rumbled. Loudly. Jack smirked and flipped on the blinker. "There's a pizza place up this road."

At the word pizza her stomach growled again. "I'd like to claim I'm not hungry, but..."

Jack laughed out loud. "Don't even try it." He swung into an open parking spot right in front of Chatham House of Pizza.

"I'll call Logan and see what he wants on his pie. We can have a beer inside while we wait."

"That sounds... really nice." Maggie smiled and Jack felt like he'd won the lottery.

25

Monday, October 14, 9:30 p.m.
23 Crosswind Farm Road, Chatham

*S*everal beers and slices of pizza later, they were back at Jack's house and finishing up with their meal. Maggie cleared the plates from the table and Logan carried the pizza boxes outside to the recycling bin. Jack leaned against the doorframe, checking email on his phone. His request to take another day's leave had been denied, probably because Jack hadn't felt safe divulging the specifics of the situation. The fewer people who knew they had the USB files, the better.

On the bright side, his captain agreed that he could meet with the representatives from the Suffolk County D.A.'s office during his shift. Since the state police barracks were also in Bourne, he'd be able to clock in and change to his official vehicle before heading to the medical examiner's office. Assistant D.A. Esposito's email sounded eager to meet and exchange information.

But what to do about Maggie?

He knew she wanted to see her sister's ghost again, but with Dr. Miller still in the hospital, any encounters would likely be more frustrating than enlightening. And until they figured out who attacked the good doctor, Maggie's life was still in danger.

More importantly... he wasn't ready to let her walk away.

"Everything okay over there?"

He looked up to catch Logan's eye. "Harper denied my request to take more time off to deal with..." he waved a hand in the air, "all this. What's your schedule this week?"

Logan caught on quickly. "Uncle Grant will let me take some time if you need me."

"Can you hang here with Maggie in the morning?"

"Sure, not a problem." Logan pulled his phone from his pocket and started texting.

"Whoa, wait a minute!" Maggie was suddenly standing in front of him. "I thought I was coming with you in the morning?"

Settling his hands on her waist, he looked her in the eye. "I'd like you to stay here with Logan tomorrow. We don't know what we're walking into up there."

"What, wait, what?" Maggie tried to wriggle away from Jack but he held firm, snaking his arms around her and holding her tight. "I need to go with you. I need to see my sister."

Jack shook his head. "It's too dangerous."

"You're not my keeper, Jack." She thumped her hands against his chest to emphasize her words. "It's not up to you to tell me what I can and can't do."

"I didn't claim to be your keeper, Maggie. But I need to keep you safe."

"Why? Because it's your *job*?" Her voice rose increasingly until she practically yelled this last question in his face.

It took everything in his power to remain calm, to stay steady in the face of her anger as he tried to explain his reasoning. "Because... I care. For some fucking inexplicable reason, I care about you. Not because you're my job, Maggie. Because you're...you."

"And on that less than eloquent note..." Logan pushed back from the desk and stood, stretching his arms toward the ceiling. "It's late. I'm headed to bed. I'll see you both in the morning." He shared one last meaningful look with Jack, one that said *Don't fuck this up*, and headed for the stairs.

Once they heard a door upstairs slam closed, Maggie's eyes met Jack's, her voice now barely a whisper. "You said that before. What does it even mean, you *care* about me?"

"Maggie..." The timing might be the worst, but the hunger for her was still there, gnawing at his insides, churning his gut.

They stood for a moment, staring into each other's eyes before he pulled her even closer, his arms taut with barely restrained need. He captured her mouth with his own, bruising her lips with a kiss that was anything but gentle as he showed her what he couldn't put into words, his desire, his hunger, his need. She inhaled deeply, sliding her hands around his neck, melting against him, pulling his head down to her as if she'd been waiting for that kiss her whole life. *His kiss.* Their tongues tangled, the intensity spiraling, her hunger seeming as great as his. *Mine*, that inner voice growled.

He backed her a few steps until she pressed to the wall, his erection hard and eager against the softness of her body. He captured her moan with his mouth, the sound sending his heart racing faster, like he'd gone over the edge of a waterfall with no way to escape the battering rocks below. One hand swept up to cradle the back of her head, angling her mouth to take it deeper. With his other hand under her bottom, he lifted her off her feet, keeping her back pinned to the wall. Instinctively she wrapped both legs around his hips and it was his turn to groan, his erection pressed directly into the juncture of her legs.

His whisper sounded more like a growl as he confirmed they were on the same page. "Is this what you want?"

"Yes." Her shaky response mirrored the need shining in her eyes. "I know this is crazy, and I know I'm in danger, but I want this. *I want you.* Even if it's just for tonight. You make me feel safe. And lo-... like you care for me."

Part of his brain registered Maggie's almost-use of the L-word, but the other part only heard her say those other important three words. *I. Want. You.*

"I will not let anything bad happen to you, Maggie Nelson."

"I know that, Jack. I trust you."

With another little growl, he captured her mouth again, moving his hands so they both cradled her bottom as he carried her down the hallway to his bedroom, kicking the door closed behind them. Bright moonlight streamed through the windows, bathing the dark room with an ethereal, other-worldly glow. He lowered her onto the bed, standing before her and tugging off his sweatshirt. He pulled off his shirt, tossing it toward the corner. Her eyes zeroed in on his bandaged upper arm, her mouth forming an adorable pout of concern before her gaze took in the rest of his chest. Heat sparked as hungry hands reached to explore, running fingernails along his abs, tracing the V that led down and disappeared into his pants. When she pressed a kiss right above the button to his jeans he couldn't control the shiver of need running through him.

Deft hands made quick work of unbuttoning his fly, pushing his boxer briefs down along with the jeans until he stood before her naked in the moonlight. She sucked in a breath, eyes wide as she took in the thick length of his rock-hard erection. She reached for him but he captured her hands, afraid he wouldn't last if she touched him.

"Your turn," he grit out, taking a small step away from the bed. He watched as she pulled her shirt over her head, revealing a lacy white bra barely restraining creamy mounds of delectable flesh. Not able to wait another moment, Jack kneeled before her and pulled her to the edge of the bed, taking one breast in hand while pressing his mouth to the other, sucking on the pebbled nipple straining through the thin lace. She gasped, her breathing shallow, every touch ratcheting them both until he reached around to unhook her bra, pulling the straps from her arms and tossing it across the room.

"Lay back," he demanded, his eyes never leaving her body, drinking in the sight of her peaked nipples and taut belly. "Maggie, you're so beautiful." With a few swift moves he removed the rest of her clothing, kicking it to the side as he kneeled before her, caressing the smooth skin of her inner thighs. She squirmed as he kissed his way from her knee up toward her center, his tongue swirling patterns on her skin, gliding closer and closer to heaven. His fingers splayed across her belly as his other hand lifted her leg to rest a knee over his shoulder so he could see her delicate folds. *Mine.*

"Oh my god, Jack..." The sound of her breathless voice speared him with need. He needed to taste her. To make her his own. He ran his tongue over her folds, finding the nub at the top and sucking it into his mouth. The hand resting on her stomach slid down toward her mound, the thumb taking over to rub her swollen clit as his tongue delved lower, exploring, slipping in and out of the crease. She bucked against him with a whimper but he held firm and slid a finger inside, feeling her inner walls clench greedily.

He pressed his tongue harder against her flesh, rewarded with more needy little noises, adding a second finger, pumping them faster as she began to throb against him, crying out his name. He kissed and sucked, loving the feel of her flesh against his tongue, loving the taste of her arousal, the slick sweetness, riding the waves of explicit pleasure right along with her, his dick aching with needs of its own.

Her body finally spent, he crawled up onto the bed next to her, staring down at her body bathed in moonlight, his throbbing cock pressed against her thigh. The look on her face sent a wave of primal satisfaction surging through him. He did that. He put that smile there. If that was all they were going to do tonight, it would be enough to see how blissed out she looked right this minute. His dick throbbed in protest but he told it to calm the fuck down. Until she opened her eyes and smiled up at him.

"What about you, Jack? Do you have a condom?" Her breathy voice sent his need spiraling again. He reached over to the bedside table and opened the drawer. Tearing the foil packet, he rolled it on quickly before covering her with his body. Eyes locked, he hovered over her, positioning himself at her opening. She bit her lip, white teeth sinking into plump flesh, and he groaned, unable to hold back a moment longer.

He speared into her wetness, and she released her bottom lip with a soft gasp as he pushed deep, filling every inch. Her body squeezed around him, still clenching with the aftershocks of her orgasm. She felt like heaven and he groaned again, and lowered his head to capture those pouty lips with his own, his kiss soft, tender, possessive. *Mine,* the voice in his head growled again. *This one is mine.*

She wrapped her arms around him, digging her fingers into the tight skin of his back, arching to press her hips forward into his. He swallowed her whimper as he slowly slid out, quickly thrusting back inside, never releasing her mouth as he pumped slowly, going deeper, further, feeling more than he had with anyone before. Sweat beaded on his forehead at the effort to keep things slow, to make it last, to make it good for her. He broke the kiss, panting to catch his breath, and her eyes opened, those forests of green filled with wonder and emotions too deep to contemplate.

"Maggie," he whispered, her name both a question and the answer all wrapped together.

"More," she whispered back as he slid out almost all the way before slamming back home. "I won't break."

Jack couldn't help but smile, pausing to plant a kiss on the tip of her nose. "You're stronger than anyone thinks."

She wriggled beneath him, arching into him. "Jack, please."

He growled his response, changing the angle by pulling one of her legs up to drape over his shoulder, before thrusting back into her warm, welcoming body. The new position must have worked for Maggie too, her eyes rolling up and back as he bumped against her inner wall. "So good," she breathed. "Oh my god, don't stop."

He pumped harder, faster, lifting her torso and hugging her against his chest now slicked with sweat. His breath became heavy and she closed her eyes, screaming his name even as her inner walls grabbed his dick, milking it as she tumbled over the edge of oblivion. Jack following close behind her, his motions unschooled and jerky in his final few thrusts, his vision blanking out until all he could see were stars shooting across the heavens. Spent, he released the leg from over his shoulder and collapsed on top of her, kissing her one last time before rolling to the side and pulling her back against his chest, fully sated.

26

Tuesday, October 15, 8:00 a.m.
Barnstable County Medical Examiner and Coroner's office, Bourne

ack pulled his state issued vehicle into the familiar parking lot, seeing that there were already a handful of cars parked near the double doors. Griff's familiar pickup was nowhere in sight. He put the vehicle into park and scrubbed a hand down his face, deciding to wait for backup before confronting the lawyers from the D.A.'s office. He needed more information about what was going on, but he wasn't sure who to trust.

Except Maggie. He trusted her. He pictured Maggie as he'd left her that morning, naked and curled up in his warm bed. It had taken all of his willpower to leave her there sleeping, but he wasn't going to risk her safety. He couldn't.

He glanced at the envelope on the passenger seat, the one

containing the USB drives. Once he'd determined whether he could trust the lawyers from Boston, he'd pass along the information they needed to help end the corruption.

One of his buddies from the force pulled up in the spot next to him, flashing a thumbs up through the window. Jack grinned back, stepping out onto the pavement and rounding the vehicle. "Tanner, am I glad to see a friendly face."

"Strength in numbers," his friend replied through the open car window. He passed Jack a handgun. "Griff told me the Worcester locals kept yours. Thought you might need another. A cop without a gun is like peanut butter without the jelly."

"Thanks." Jack took the offered weapon, pondering his friend's analogy and wondering if he was supposed to be the peanut butter in the situation. His thoughts were interrupted by Sister Sledge belting out the ringtone indicting Cameron was calling. Or rather, Dan. Jack shoved the gun into his jacket pocket and answered immediately.

"Maggie, we need to talk this through. You can't give your sister's ledger to the District Attorney." Dan sounded anxious. "I know they traveled down to the Cape this morning. You can't meet with them."

"Good morning to you too, Mr. Koslov." Jack heard the other man's sharp intake of breath. He nodded one last time to Tanner and began walking toward the brick building as he spoke with Dan.

"Who is this?"

"This is Maggie's friend, the one you shot on Sunday? What I'd like to know is why. What could be so important in that ledger that it's worth shooting people? Is it the videos?"

Silence stretched between them for a beat. Finally Dan asked, "You watched the tapes?"

"Yes," Jack lied. "What I don't understand is why you'd be willing to risk jail time to protect any of those guys."

"You don't understand. These guys are powerful. I'm just a small cog in the vast political machine."

"Soon to be a small cog in the prison system."

Another long pause. "I'm not going to prison for them."

"You could testify against them. Be a whistleblower." Jack didn't know if that kind of offer would even be valid once the D.A. got his hands on the information, but it felt like the right thing to offer. He'd reached the double doors, and turned to face the parking lot. Tipping his face to the sun, he closed his eyes and savored the warm heat and the salty breeze, waiting for Dan to make the right choice.

After several contemplative seconds, Dan barked a laugh at him. "Cameron was the original whistleblower, you know. She turned herself in when she realized what was really going on. And look what happened to her."

Jack squeezed his eyes tighter, not liking the taste of his next lie. "The D.A. can keep you safe."

"Like they did with Cameron? With A.D.A. Kazinski? With your coroner?" Dan's laugh sounded hollow. "I don't think that's an option."

"Then what do you want?"

More silence. Until Jack heard the click of a gun being cocked. He opened his eyes and found Dan emerging from one of the parked cars near the entrance, a few yards from where Jack stood. His gun pointed at Jack. "Give me the evidence, Jack, and no one gets hurt."

"All right, all right. You already shot me once this week..." Jack let his words trail off as he made a show of reaching into his pocket as if to hand over the information. Instead he whipped out the gun and pointed it at Dan. "Put the gun down, Mr. Koslov. No one needs to get hurt today."

"Someone always gets hurt," Dan countered, a smirk on his face. "Why should today be any different?"

27

Tuesday, October 15, 8:00 a.m.
23 Crosswind Farm Road, Chatham

An uneasy dream roused her, her eyelids heavy and unwilling to open, probably due to her sleep deficit over the last few days. And then last night... Maggie's lips stretched into a smile as images of Jack's naked body flit through her head, chasing away the remnants of her nightmare. She had no idea sex could be so completely earthshattering. Like Jack had literally shattered her world into pieces and rearranged them in a new formation that included him.

Like he was the missing piece to the puzzle of her life.

Maggie snaked her fingers across the soft sheet, searching for Jack, but found his pillow already cold. Cracking one eye, she saw she was alone in the room. Propping up on her elbows, she focused on a nearby clock. Eight in the morning. Still early.

So where was Jack? Bathroom? Kitchen? Out for a morning run? She realized she had no idea what his morning routine entailed, or even if he was a morning person or a night owl.

She barely knew him, and yet she'd slept with him. That fact alone should have her hiding under the covers for the rest of the day, embarrassed by her brazen behavior. Instead, she stretched out in his bed like a contented feline, a silly grin claiming her face.

She'd waited far too long to find someone like Jack. Sweet, sensitive, and sexy as hell. Protective and trustworthy. Everything she could want and so much more. Now that she'd found him, she was jumping in with both feet, eyes wide open.

Her bag still in the guest room, she pulled on her underwear and jeans from the day before and snagged one of Jack's shirts from his closet. In the adjoining bathroom, she found a fresh washcloth and hand towel in the linen closet and scrubbed her face. She stared at her reflection, wondering how her face could look the same when so much had happened. The eyes staring back at her from the mirror looked the same as ever, but she felt like a different person.

It wasn't just the shooting and the political intrigue, not only the ghost... but Jack. Meeting Jack. Talking to Jack. Being with Jack. She was still herself, still Maggie Nelson, but different. Changed, after seeing herself through his eyes.

And she liked this new self.

He'd said last night that she was stronger than anyone thought. She wanted to believe that was true, that it was all her, but she was pretty sure it was being with Jack that made the difference.

Hanging the used towel and washcloth over the edge of the sink to dry, she wandered down the hall. The heavenly scent of rich, dark coffee led her to the kitchen, where she found Logan.

The mountain of a man leaned against the counter reading a newspaper, coffee mug in hand. *Wrong brother*, and she bit back her disappointment. Logan seemed like a nice guy, despite his huge size. He might be too tall and too broad in the shoulders for her taste, but he was well-proportioned, with a sharp wit and a handsome face.

She saw the resemblance to Jack, even though it wasn't nearly the same as the way she and Cameron looked alike. Logan was definitely the kind of guy she'd choose to be friends with. Well, if she ever chose to have friends who were guys. Friends in general were something her life lacked at the moment. She cleared her throat to rid it of the sticky, unwanted emotions.

He glanced up at the sound. "Good morning, Mags. Ready for some coffee?" He gestured toward the half full pot on the counter where an empty mug stood waiting for her.

"A man after my own heart," she said, pouring a cup of the dark, aromatic brew.

Logan chuckled. "Don't let my brother hear you say that. I like my testicles where they are, thank you very much."

She chuckled even as her cheeks heated at the off-color joke. "I, uh, hope we didn't keep you awake last night."

"No worries. I was listening to an audiobook as usual. With headphones of course."

Awkward. Her cheeks heated further, dwelling on the fact that this was apparently the *usual*. What she'd thought was earthshattering was merely a one-night stand to a guy like Jack. A guy that hot probably had a different girl in his bed every weekend. Tears pricked behind her eyes, but she blinked them back. "Oh. Good. I mean, I guess you're used to this sort of thing?"

It took Logan a beat to process her words. His eyes

widened and he gave a quick shake of his head. "Uh, no, actually. Jack never brings anyone home. Ever. He hasn't had a girlfriend, or anyone he really cares about, in the last four years."

"But… you said the audiobook thing is your usual…"

Logan laughed and shook his head. "Yes, audiobooks are my usual thing at night to help me relax. Jack used to get on my case about the noise and gave me headphones last year for Christmas. I didn't mean to imply you two were overly loud or anything like that."

Her mortification must have been evident because Logan took pity on her, his face softening. "My brother's a really good guy, Maggie. I hope things work out between you."

"Um, yeah. Thanks. Speaking of your brother, though, where is Jack?"

Logan took another long sip, eyeing her over the edge of his mug. Eventually, he said, "Jack headed up to Bourne about an hour ago, taking the files up to the Medical Examiner's office to meet with the D.A."

Coffee sloshed over the rim of the mug, splashing down her front. "Without me?"

"Maggie, he did what he though was best." Logan placed his cup on the counter and folded his newspaper. "Besides, he said you complained about being on Cape Cod and not seeing the ocean at all. I thought we could take a walk down the hill and visit my aunt. She and Uncle Grant live right on the shores of Pleasant Bay."

"But… but…" Maggie struggled with what she wanted to say. She'd worried about seeing the officials from the D.A.'s office, and worried Dan would try to find her, but at the same time, this was her life. Cameron was her sister and Maggie needed to stand up and do the right thing. Jack effectively took the decision away from her, leaving her stranded in Chatham while he went to deal with her mess.

The look on Logan's face was infinitely kind and understanding. "He cares about you, Mags. He's only trying to protect you."

She drew in a deep breath and blew it out slowly, counting the beats of her heart, willing it to slow. "Who's going to protect him? The police in Worcester kept his gun."

"He called a few of his buddies from the force to meet him at the county building," Logan explained. "Strength in numbers. See, he thought of everything."

Not everything. "What about letting me say good-bye to my sister before they take her body up to Boston?"

Logan's face softened further. "Mags, your sister is gone. You saw her yesterday. Nothing changed overnight."

She forgot Logan didn't know about Cameron's ghost. But Jack knew. And made the decision for her, regardless of her feelings. It might be the last chance she'd ever have to see her sister. The doctor told them the other day that ghosts stuck around to resolve their problems. If Jack and the D.A. took care of things, Cameron would move on and Maggie would never see her again.

Jack hadn't considered that, or given her the option to accompany him. To say one last good-bye. Probably because – after everything that happened – the man still didn't believe in ghosts.

"I'm cooking eggs and toast for breakfast. Why don't you take a quick shower and join me when you're done?" Logan moved closer, gently laying one of his giant paws on her shoulder. "We'll eat and then head to the beach. Sound good?"

Maggie nodded, her brain still buzzing with hurt as she retreated down the hall. At the last minute she detoured to grab her duffle bag, feeling like fresh underwear would probably be a good thing after her shower. New underwear would help make everything feel a little more normal.

A quick shower helped put her world back into perspective, although the scent of Jack's soap made her miss him and wish he hadn't left her asleep in bed. Wish he'd given her a choice. Wish for more than a one-night stand. One night together would never be enough.

She wondered if Jack felt the same way.

But if he did, would he have left her like this? Without waking her, talking to her, asking what it was she wanted? Maybe Logan was wrong, and it really was just a weekend fling for him. One night of fucking to get it out of their systems. If that was the case, could she handle it? The thought gave her pause. She took a deep breath. Could she relegate what happened to the category of "just sex between consenting adults," even though she knew in her heart it was so much more?

By the time she emerged from the bathroom, she'd pulled on her proverbial big girl panties and pushed all of her feelings into a little box, determined not to think about them again until she was back in Worcester, safe in her own bed with all of this a hazy memory in her rearview mirror.

True to his promise, Logan cooked up a delicious breakfast, adding herbs to scrambled eggs along with toast from a loaf of locally baked ciabatta bread. Maggie helped him clean the disaster he'd made of the kitchen before they left the house, heading down a long, graveled driveway. As they neared the main road, the trees cleared and across the way she saw a wide swath of ocean winking at them under a cloudless blue sky. She stopped for a moment to take in the view.

Logan continued a few steps before realizing she was no longer at his side. "Everything okay?"

"This is gorgeous." She took a deep breath, tasting the salty tang on her lips, on her tongue. Bright sunshine sparkled on the water, like so many stars fallen to earth. A large landscaping truck rumbled by, breaking the spell with loud music, wafting the scent of fresh-mown grass in its wake, reminding her they were in a real place and not in some fantasy world. "Jack told me you guys grew up here?"

Logan nodded. "Yeah, it can be a pretty cool place to live. Summer can be crazy with so many tourists flooding the area, but perfect blue-sky days like this make it all seem worth it." He smiled at her. "Come on. Let's cross the street to the beach. You can dip your toes in the water."

"Wait, let me take a picture of this view first." She reached for her phone before remembering she didn't have it with her. "Shoot, I forgot my cell phone. Can we go back for it?"

Logan looked uncomfortable. "Jack took it with him this morning. He didn't want Dan tracking you to the house while he was in Bourne."

"He...what?" The discussion flooded back to her, how Dan might be using Cameron's phone to find Maggie. "But I turned it off. Didn't he trust me?"

"You were about to turn it on to take a picture," Logan pointed out. "Mags, he trusts you or he wouldn't have left you here with me. Like I said before, my brother cares about you. He wants you safe."

"Safe," Maggie repeated, trying to process the swirl of emotions and feelings Jack stirred inside her with his every move.

A burst of music punctuated the crisp morning air. Logan frowned, digging into his pocket for his cell phone, grimacing at the screen before punching the button. "Hello?" Maggie watched as the color drained from the big man's face. "Okay. We'll be there as soon as we can." He shoved the phone back in his jeans and grabbed Maggie's hand. "Change of plans. We need to go."

"Go where?" Maggie hurried to keep up with Logan's longer strides.

"Falmouth hospital. Jack's been shot."

28

Tuesday, October 15
Falmouth Hospital, 100 Ter Heun Drive, Falmouth

*J*ack sat up, disoriented, his eyes unable to focus for the first few moments with the lights so bright. A high pitched ringing filled his ears. He knew there were people all around him, he could feel that they were there, but he couldn't see or hear anything through the blinding light. Not the people. Not his surroundings. Nothing.

How can light be so loud?

"Jack. Can you hear me?"

The voice sounded familiar but he couldn't place it. He turned toward the sound, his eyes finally focusing on the face he'd hoped to see. The most beautiful woman he'd ever met. "Maggie! Thank God you're here. What happened? Where am I?"

There was something wrong with her eyes... they looked grey instead of the emerald green he'd come to love. *Love.* He should have told her last night how he felt. That he was falling in love with her. It was too soon, too sudden, too real... he'd never felt this way before. He should say something. But what if she didn't feel the same way? How did he know if this feeling was love? How could he be sure she'd love him back?

Indecision clawed his insides. Before he could decide what to do, she spoke.

"Jack, I'm Cameron. Not Maggie."

He frowned at her words. "That can't be right. Cameron is..."

"Dead. A ghost. Even though you don't believe in us." Her smile looked achingly sad.

Horror jolted through him like an electric shock. "I don't believe in ghosts. We studied all the philosophers in college. Descartes theories of mind body duality were proven wrong."

She raised one eyebrow. "And yet here we are."

"Does that mean I'm..."

"Not yet. You still have the choice to go back."

Shock zipped through his body again at her words. *Choice.* Green eyes filled his thoughts. He wanted to choose Maggie. To be with her forever. After so few days, could she possibly feel the same way about him?

"Before you leave, I need to know. Do you love my sister?"

He focused on Cameron, so much like the woman he loved... except for the sad look on her face and those grey eyes, looking at him expectantly, waiting for his answer.

Did he love Maggie? The question that seemed difficult to answer just moments before seemed so simple now.

"Yes. I love her."

Cameron nodded, even as her entire body began to fade.

"Good. She deserves to be happy. Keep her safe from Dan and the Russians."

Jack winced. "Dan shouldn't be a problem anymore. I shot him before he shot me."

"Good." Cameron's eyes blazed with righteous anger. "He worked directly for Governor Plunkett. He's got a few Russian mobsters on his payroll too. Make sure all of them are stopped."

"We found the USB sticks you hid with your sister." *Maggie.* Just the thought of her sent a jolt through his system. "How do I know if she loves me?"

"If you love her you need to tell her. Love means taking that leap into the unknown. Hopefully it's not a journey you take alone, like mine." Her entire body began to fade.

"Wait, where are you going?"

"I'm not going anywhere, I'm already here. You're the one who needs to go back." The light surrounding them brightened, her outline fading as everything turned to white and another shock zipped through his body.

Then everything went black.

29

Tuesday, October 15, 2:30 p.m.
Falmouth Hospital, 100 Ter Heun Drive, Falmouth

The hard plastic chairs in the small waiting area offered little comfort to the family and friends gathered to wait for news of Jack's surgery. Maggie sat alone in the corner she'd occupied the day before, when she'd been here *with* Jack and not *because* of him. She made silent deals with Heaven. *Please just let Jack survive*, she pleaded. *He has so many people who love him and need him. I need him. He has to be okay. I'll do whatever you want, just let him be okay.*

When she and Logan first arrived at the hospital, only Jack's parents paced back and forth in the small waiting room. Luckily no ghosts hovered nearby. Just the parents of the man she loved.

Loved.

She loved him. And now she might lose him without ever getting the chance to tell him.

She watched as Logan wrapped each parent in a tight embrace before taking a few moments to introduce Maggie. Patrick and Louise MacDonald were kind, but understandably distracted by the circumstances. Maybe being back here in the hospital was just as hard for them as it had been for Jack the day before. Except now their oldest son was in surgery, fighting for his life.

Wanting to feel useful, Maggie used the skills she'd honed at the diner and took coffee orders. In her mind, coffee made everything more bearable. Plus, it gave her something to occupy her mind and her hands. By the time she found the hospital cafeteria and returned with drinks and assorted snacks, more family arrived. Aunts, uncles, and two of Jack and Logan's cousins, both tall, good-looking guys. Again, Maggie took orders and made another trip downstairs to the cafeteria. When she returned a second time with a tray of assorted drinks, the remaining uncle had arrived, apologizing that his wife Ann was stuck at a school event.

The waiting area seemed even smaller with almost a dozen family members milling around, speaking in low tones and texting with the family members who weren't present. Several of Jack's fellow officers dropped in and out, checking for news. One of them introduced himself to her as Griffin when she offered him a can of soda, saying he was Jack's partner.

Not wanting to bother Logan, she introduced herself by first name to the family members as she offered to bring them something from the cafeteria. She knew from her conversation with Jack that Dylan was some sort of retired investment banker, but Maggie didn't think he looked anywhere near old enough to already be retired. Ed was a detective on the

Chatham police force and seemed to be the calmest one in the room, reassuring Jack's parents that everything would be fine. Sporadic updates from the surgical team liaison sounded promising. Finally, one of the doctors came out and spoke in low tones with Jack's parents, good news judging from his mother's smile, paired with happy tears.

Sitting in the corner, Maggie wondered what it would be like to be part of such a large, caring family. It wasn't something she'd ever wanted before, but sitting here, watching everyone hug and share and cry together, made her ache for that feeling of belonging. She hoped Jack appreciated all the people he had pulling for him. If the situation was reversed, if she'd gone with him to Bourne... if she'd been the one who'd been shot... who would be in the waiting room for her?

No one.

Guilt racked her conscience at the turn of her thoughts and the envy she felt. Despite her relief that Jack was going to be okay, she felt lonely. Alone. She wished things were different. That she'd met this family in some normal way, and could be part of their celebration now.

"Are you Maggie? Maggie Nelson?"

She looked up to find Jack's partner Griff standing over her, hands on his hips, a puzzled smile on his face.

"That's me."

"Hey, I know you introduced yourself earlier when you gave me the Pepsi, but for some reason I thought you worked here at the hospital. It just dawned on me you might be the Maggie that Jack told me about."

A light sparked inside her at his words. "Jack mentioned me?"

Griff sat down in the seat next to hers. "I'm sorry about your sister. I was with Jack when we found her body."

The light inside her dimmed at the reminder of why she was truly here on Cape Cod. The reason she'd met Jack in the first place. She sucked in a breath and sat straighter. "Jack called you to meet him at the Medical Examiner's office this morning, right? Were you there... when the shooting happened?"

He shook his head. "Arrived a little too late, which is going to keep me up nights for a while, I'm sure. But the good news is Jack will be okay."

Questions raced through her mind, wanting to know who shot Jack and what it had to do with her sister...if the USB drives were safe, if Dan was involved... but before she could formulate what she wanted to ask, he stood and offered her a hand. "I have to get back to the M.E.'s office if you'd like a lift. I can fill you in on the details while we're driving to Bourne. I'm sure someone from the District Attorney's office can give you a ride the rest of the way back to Boston."

She froze as his words slowly sank in. He'd give her a ride. Because the family wasn't going to leave for a while, not until they could see Jack for themselves. If she took Griff's offer she wouldn't have to be a bother to Logan, or scramble for a way to get back to Boston. Or Worcester.

But she wanted to see Jack. See for herself he was okay. At least say goodbye to him.

Jack who was shot – again – because of her.

She glanced around the crowded room, noting the arrival of even more family. One of Jack's hunky cousins was now hugging a beautiful brunette who looked a lot like Priyanka Chopra. The doctor was ushering Logan and his parents down the hall toward the recovery room.

Jack had family to support him. He didn't need his one-night-stand sticking around like she thought she belonged here. Like last night meant something more than sex. He certainly didn't need her heaping any more trouble onto his plate. She'd done quite enough. In all of her bargaining with the Heavens for Jack to be okay, she said she'd do anything. Even walk away if she needed to.

She met Griff's eyes again. "Sure, a ride would be great."

CHAPTER 30

Two weeks later
Halloween, 8:30 p.m.
Mike's Diner, the corner of Green Street and Main, Worcester

$\mathcal{M}$aggie wasn't in the mood to wait on one more drunken frat boy, but staring at the clock wouldn't make her shift end any faster. She wanted to get out of here, back to her apartment. Her roommates would all be out partying, which was fine with her. Having some time alone to think would probably be a good thing.

She needed to figure out what she wanted to do about Jack.

They hadn't spoken since before the shooting. When she'd gotten her phone back from the detectives investigating the incident, she saw several missed calls from Jack. He most likely forgot how he'd confiscated her cell before running off on his own to confront the bad guys. The sound of his voice in the sweet messages he left put a lump in her throat the size of Mount Rushmore.

How could she talk to him? He almost died. Because of her.

But then Jack started texting. *Don't know why you won't talk to me, but I miss you Maggie.*

Short, sweet, and tear jerking. She'd stared at that message for an hour, her thumb hovering over the delete button. She couldn't bring herself to do it. She also didn't know what to type in return. So she didn't.

The next text came a day later. Maggie was in Cambridge, making arrangements for Cameron's burial. No point in having a big funeral. Maggie was the only Nelson left to grieve. She sat in the offices at Mount Auburn Cemetery and read Jack's words at least fifty time. *The DA called. He has your sister's files, and a lead on who killed her. Arrests should come soon. I miss you.*

The next day's text was lighter in nature. *The doctor told me to stay away from caffeine. I told him coffee solves all life's problems in one delightful little cup. I miss you.* She laughed at his use of her favorite quote from Mike's Diner. After staring at the screen for a few minutes, she texted back.

I miss you too.

Which opened the floodgates, so to speak, and they'd been texting back and forth since then. He offered to come to Boston to be with her at the burial. She declined. She asked him for details about what happened that day in Bourne. He told her. He also told her about his recovery, about his hovering family driving him crazy, about his niece dragging him to the weekend harvest festival on Chatham's Main Street the minute he was released from the hospital. She told him about her interview at the D.A.'s office. About her plans to put the brownstone on the market. About getting extensions on the midterms she'd missed because of everything else going on.

Not once did either of them bring up what happened between them that night in Chatham, although Maggie was starting to think she needed to say something. The truth was she missed him with an intensity that shocked her. How did he become so essential in such a short period of time?

But what was it she wanted to say? What did she want to do about it?

She lived in Worcester and had another semester and a half until graduation.

He lived in Chatham, with a house and a family and a career.

They'd had one weekend together. One night of bliss. Was it enough for either of them to change their worlds?

One night. But it felt like so much more. Did that make her a clingy, silly female? Probably. And yet here it was two weeks later and he still consumed most of her waking thoughts. And definitely all of her dreams.

She hefted the fresh pitcher of water and made her way to the table of six in the corner. One of the other waitresses tapped her on the shoulder, looking as harried as Maggie felt. "There's a guy up front who insists on being seated in your section. I told him all your tables were full, but he says he'll wait."

Maggie frowned. "He asked for me specifically?"

"By name, sweetie. Do you have a date after work?"

A brief thought of Jack flit through her head but she pushed it away. "No."

"Well then maybe I'll ask him out. He's pretty yummy, and he's waiting out by the register if you want to talk to him." Message delivered, the blonde turned away to her own tables, leaving Maggie frowning over the pitcher of water.

Who'd be looking for her here at the diner? Maybe it had something to do with Cameron. She called back to the other wait-ress. "Wait, Sally, is he a cop?"

"That's part of the yummy. I love a man in uniform." Sally winked before walking away.

A cop. Made sense. It'd been two weeks since Cameron's murder, and a week since she'd buried her sister alongside their parents. Maybe it was someone following up.

She finished pouring waters for the table of six, dropped a check for her party of four, and asked a few other tables if they were all set before her curiosity got the better of her. Rounding the corner, she stopped dead in her tracks.

Jack MacDonald.

His head down studying the menu, he didn't notice her right away and she took the few moments to drink in the sight of him. Tall and just as devastatingly handsome as in her memo-ries, he looked thinner than she remembered, his cheeks hollow. The state trooper uniform hid his body from her, and she wondered how he could be back at work so soon after being shot? More important, what he was doing here, so far from home?

He looked up, those true blue eyes locking with hers, spearing into her soul with a force that felt like a physical blow, rocking her back a step. He stood taller but didn't make a move, as if he wasn't sure she was real, or was afraid to scare her away. Tentatively, she crept closer, step by step until she was standing in front of him.

"Hi." She breathed in his scent and the knot in her stomach unclenched.

"Hi," he repeated, his husky voice sending goosebumps down her arms.

She cleared her throat, trying to clear the cobwebs from her brain as well. "I heard you were asking for me."

"I did." He continued to stare into her eyes, as if they held all the answers to the universe.

She shifted under his intense gaze, keeping her tone neutral. "How've you been?"

"I started back on desk duty yesterday. Even if I wasn't physically recovering from the shooting, I'd be on desk duty for shooting Dan." His eyes searched hers again. "I'm sorry I killed your friend."

"He wasn't my friend," Maggie said quickly.

He nodded once, never releasing his hold on her eyes. "I need to know why you left the hospital that day. I asked for you when I woke, but you'd gone. I thought maybe it was because I'd killed him."

She shifted again, uncomfortable under his penetrating gaze. "I didn't even know about that until later. And no, if it was a choice between you and him, I'm glad you are the one who survived."

He lowered his eyes. "I'm sorry I missed your sister's burial."

"No worries. You said that in your text."

"I wish I'd been there for you."

"Why? Obviously, I'm not good for your health. You were shot twice in the weekend we were together."

Both corners of Jack's mouth quirked up. "Totally worth it. I'd do it all again in a heartbeat."

Her hands fisted on her hips to keep from shaking. "Really? Getting shot was that much fun?"

His eyes blazed a trail down her body that felt like a physical caress. "Kissing you most definitely was." His voice lowered. "Why'd you leave?"

She exhaled the breath she'd been holding, trying to ignore the flames licking her skin. "Jack, what do you want from me?"

"To see you. We need to talk."

Her eyes landed on Sally watching her from across the way. "I can't do this right now. I'm working."

"I know. I'll wait. We can talk after your shift is over."

"I'm here until ten o'clock," she warned him.

"That's okay. I hear you've got good coffee here."

Maggie smiled, feeling her heart lighten. "Coffee isn't actually a food group, you know."

"Bite your tongue!" Jack smiled back at her, parroting her words from two weeks earlier. "Coffee solves all life's problems in one delightful little cup." He jerked a thumb at one of the signs behind the counter, which proclaimed that same phrase. "I never realized you were quoting Jerry Seinfeld."

She laughed. "Good answer. I may even let you walk me home after work."

His eyes blazed with intention. "I'm counting on it."

"Why, Jack?"

He took a step closer, his heat invading her senses. His hands planted on her hips, pulling her closer. "Maggie, the day I was shot..."

One eyebrow quirked up. "The first time or the second time?"

"The first time doesn't count. That was only a scratch," Jack scoffed, barely concealing his grin. His face sobered again quickly. "There was a point during the surgery that my heart stopped beating. The doc said I was technically dead for several moments. They used a defibrillator to bring me back."

Tears filled her eyes at the thought. "See, right there. *That* was my fault. That's why I left the hospital. I'm not good for you."

His arms snaked around to hold her tight. "No, Dan Koslov was the one who shot me. Governor Plunkett's team are the ones to blame, with the whole blackmailing scheme to crush his political rivals."

"I read about that in the newspaper," she whispered, trying to focus on his words but distracted by his warm arms around her middle and his firm hands on her backside.

"Those few seconds in the light made me realize I don't want to waste any more time. Life is too short to not put all your cards on the table and go for what you want. And Maggie, I want you."

She gasped, a tear escaping and rolling down her cheek. He took advantage of her parted lips and covered them with his own, his kiss hard and hungry. She returned his kiss with a ferocity that surprised her. Too soon, the sound of a throat being cleared startled them apart. In a kiss-induced haze, Maggie saw her coworker standing next to them, a huge grin on her face. Cheeks burning, she apologized. "Sorry, Sally. I'll get back to work right away."

The blonde waved off her words. "Why don't you go clock out? I'll finish up with your tables. Looks like you and your state trooper have a little catching up to do."

Maggie grinned and caught Jack's returning smile. "Yes, yes we do."

EPILOGUE

*E*ight weeks later
   Friday, December 20, 4:25 p.m.
Hyannis Transportation Center, Main Street, Hyannis

He paced the waiting area, impatient for the arrival of the bus. He stopped in front of the news stand and scanned the headlines.

SEX SCANDAL ENGULFS STATE HOUSE

PRESIDENTIAL HOPEFUL FACES
48 COUNTS OF RACKETEERING

BOOBS, BRIBERY + BLACKMAIL

PLUNKETT'S PLAN FOR PREZ PLUMMET

He nodded to himself at the headlines. It had certainly taken long enough for the D.A.'s office to jump through all the legal hoops required to nail Governor Plunkett. Personally, he thought the blackmail tapes spoke for themselves.

If only the grand jury could accept testimony from a ghost.

And yes, Jack would readily admit the existence of ghosts. He had to accept the fact, now that he'd almost been one himself.

But he wasn't. He chose life. And Maggie. Whose bus should arrive any moment.

Convincing Maggie to spend winter break on Cape Cod had been easy, but getting her to agree to spend the actual Christmas holidays with his family took a little more effort. She'd been overwhelmed at Thanksgiving by the crowd at Aunt Ann's farmhouse, with all of his aunts and uncles and most of his cousins and their respective girlfriends in attendance.

It seemed like she'd bonded a bit with Dylan's girlfriend Bella, which was a good thing. He needed her to make friends if he wanted to convince her to stay... to move in with him after she graduated in May. He'd already spoken with Logan about buying out his half of the house... and put a deposit on a diamond ring at Chatham Jewelers to seal the deal.

His cousins seemed to think he was rushing things, but being shot put things into a different perspective. Almost dying on the operating table and meeting Cameron's ghost made him rethink everything. Descartes might have been right on the money with his ideas of mind-body duality. Because ghosts certainly did exist. But the more important realization was that he loved Maggie.

And life is too short to waste on indecision.

With his philosophical ideas turned upside down, Jack spent a lot of his recent downtime rereading his old college textbooks. His favorite philosopher was now Aristotle, who famously wrote that "Love is comprised of a single soul inhabiting two bodies." Which, he realized, is how he felt from the moment he met Maggie that fateful October day.

She was the missing piece to his puzzle. And he was never losing her again.

ALSO BY KATIE O'SULLIVAN

Cape Cod Dating Rules series:

Breaking the Rules, Book 1

Bending the Rules, Book 2

Changing the Rules, Book 3

Cape Cod Dating Rules: a paperback collection of all 3 stories

Hot Hunks ~ Steamy Romance series:

Quinn's Resolution (*a Cape Cod romance*)

Brendan's Christmas Surprise (*a Cape Cod romance*)

Ed's Blind Date Dilemma (*a Cape Cod romance*)

My Everyday Hero: Logan (*a Cape Cod romance*)

Wild Rose Press:

My Kind Of Crazy

Crazy About You (also in Audiobook)

Say Yes (*a Candy Hearts romance*)

Ghosts Don't Lie

Wicked Whale Publishing:

Descent, Book 1

Defiance, Book 2

Deception, Book 3

Destiny, Book 4 (*coming soon*)

ABOUT THE AUTHOR

Katie O'Sullivan is an award-winning writer with over a dozen contemporary romance and young adult books to her name.

A voracious reader, she loves to read and write second chance stories with strong female characters and hot alpha males. A recovering English major, she earned her degree at Colgate University and now lives on Cape Cod with her family and big dogs, drinking way too much coffee and finding new uses for all the sea glass she obsessively collects from the beach right down the road. She writes YA and romantic suspense novels, as well as working full time for a high tech company. Which explains all the coffee.

Find her on Facebook at Author Katie O'Sullivan
Follow her on Instagram at Cape Cod Katie
Find her on Bookbub at Katie O'Sullivan
Follow her on Twitter at OKatieO
Check out her website at www.katie-osullivan.com

Books are available online and in stores.

WANT MORE?

Quinn MacDonald had it made. With a record label deal and their first single skyrocketing up the charts, his indie punk band is finally getting a taste of rock and roll fame. Bikini-clad women and bottomless bottles of booze fill endless days... until their hotel collapses during a hurricane. He's still under contract but as far as he's concerned, the music died along with the rest of his band.

Life has never been easy for Phoebe Snow. Working three minimum wage jobs barely keeps a roof over her head while she and her band struggle to get noticed. But on stage, nothing matters but the music in her heart. When her band plays a cover of one of his hits, Quinn is blown away. Can Phoebe be the inspiration he needs for more than just writing songs?

Excerpt from *Quinn's Resolution*, published 2019 from Windmill Point Publishing:

Monday, November 28, 2016
Pandawa Beach, Bali

"And...cut! That's a wrap for the day, people. Can we get those boys some towels?"

Quinn MacDonald shook the salt water out of his hair, listening to the director yell at the crew. He knew he looked like a sheepdog shaking the water from his tangle of shoulder length curls, but at this point he didn't give a flying fuck.

He was hot. He was tired. And he needed a fucking beer.

Shooting music videos on a tropical beach sounded a helluva lot more fun when their manager pitched it back in London, where November had been miserably wet and cold.

Reality had him and his bandmates knee-deep in turquoise salt water under the relentless sun, banging on fake instruments for hours on end... well, all except Grubber who insisted on bringing his Gibson out into the ocean with him. Quinn's throat blazed from screaming out lyrics all afternoon. He knew the final video would be overdubbed to cut out the crowd noises from the beach, but it wouldn't look real unless he was actually singing.

Meanwhile the prima donna actor-turned-director kept taking breaks to flirt with anyone with boobs and sign autographs for gawking tourists, leaving the band standing in the ocean, and slowing the entire fucking process to a snail's pace.

Not that Quinn knew anything about making a music video. This was the band's first. They were a punk band, for fuck's sake. Music videos were for sellouts, right? Except their record company deemed it necessary, and their manager pointed out that Green Day even made a Broadway musical out of one of their albums.

So here they were.

Bali.

Like anyone in their right mind would complain about being on a tropical island surrounded by hot chicks in bikinis. Quinn's mind drifted to the woman in his bed the night before. Blonde with big boobs and a luscious German accent. Sabina? Sofia? Whatever the fuck her name was, she was a screamer. That part he remembered.

A giant splash caught Quinn off balance. "Dude, watch it!" He glared at Chuck Bellamy, his best friend since freshman orientation at Boston College, currently using his fake bass guitar like a paddle, splashing the hell out of the rest of them. George Hastings, who they still called "Grubber" from their rugby days, was cursing him out, trying to keep his precious Gibson dry. Chuck cackled at him and turned to attack the drummer, John Hayes, the two of them getting into a full-on water fight like five-year-olds on a sugar high.

Quinn's annoyance faded as he watched them having fun. *Fuck it. We're in Bali.* He joined the melee, leaping onto Grubber's back and pulling him under the salty water, guitar and all.

The four met on the rugby field when Chuck and Quinn were freshmen and the other two were sophomores. The band's name, Dead Ball Line, was the rugby term for out-of-bounds. It had been a goof at first, playing Green Day and Blink 182 covers at fraternity parties, pretending at being rock stars to score chicks. It wasn't until they moved to London after Grubber's graduation that they started adding Quinn's original songs into the mix.

And now here they were on a tropical island, surrounded by gorgeous women in bikinis, shooting a music video for the album they'd finished recording last month. Quinn wrote each and every song on the album, relying on Grubber to flesh out the tunes and John to create the fast beat their fans craved.

If the success of the first single, *No More Tomorrows*, was any indication, the album would do well.

They'd finally made it.

Life was good.

"Great shoot today, Quinn."

Oliver Brown fell in step next to Quinn. Twenty years older than the band, he'd been assigned by the record label to keep them on task. In the ten short months he'd been with Dead Ball

Line, Quinn grew to respect the guy. British to the core, Oliver never lost his cool or showed too much emotion. His disapproving frown was enough to keep the guys in line at the studio, and he knew better than to restrict the band's "after hours" activities. *Boys will be boys*, he'd say with one eyebrow raised. As long as they didn't break any laws, Oliver left them to it.

The group trudged up the beach toward the hospitality tent to grab more towels and knock back a few beers. The water fight got a little out of hand, dragging several bikini-clad bystanders into the fray, as well as some of the film crew. After a long hot day in the sun, they'd all needed the release. Except, perhaps, the prima donna director, who was nowhere to be seen. Oliver said he'd hightailed it back to his swanky hotel on the other side of the island.

One of those bikini-clad tourists currently molded her body against Quinn, her arm wrapped possessively around his waist. She eyed Oliver warily, like he might try to take away her new toy. Quinn almost laughed out loud, but instead smiled and patted the generous curves of her bottom. "Why don't you run ahead to the party tent and grab us some drinks, sweetheart. I'll be along in a minute."

She stepped in front of him and cupped his cheeks with both hands, pressing an open mouth kiss to his lips. "Don't keep me waiting, *mon cher*." She turned and sashayed ahead of them, hips swaying with a hypnotizing rhythm.

Both Quinn and Oliver stood transfixed for several moments. "French?" Oliver finally asked, breaking the spell.

"Swiss, actually." Quinn smiled, digging his toes into the warm sand. "The French chick was two nights ago. Old news. So what's the good word on the single, Ollie?" The new Billboard rankings released every Tuesday but with the sixteen hour time difference between Bali and Los Angeles, Quinn knew there would be nothing definitive until late the next day.

Except for the fact that Oliver always seemed to have an inside track.

"Still climbing steady. *No More Tomorrows* should definitely be in the top fifty this week. Fingers crossed, of course."

"When we hit the top ten, do we get an upgrade for our hotel rooms? Maybe we could all stay at that fucking palace where the director is camped out." Not that Quinn was actually complaining. The rooms were a step up from their shared flat in London, and the hotel's location was close to the beach and bars, with nightclubs both on the roof and in the basement. With the band's party-boy reputation, the label would've been crazy to house them somewhere expensive. Ten months ago, Quinn would've called his friends normal twenty-somethings. Since signing the contract with the record studio, they'd amped up their partying to an eleven, to the point where their bar bills exceeded their share of the take at every show they played, and their landlord was ready to kick them out of the building for violating the neighborhood's late-night noise restrictions.

And the women… it seemed crazy to Quinn that women who didn't know him wanted to jump in his bed because he was in a band. Granted, that's why they started the band in the first place back in college, but he'd never thought it would be this easy.

Speaking of which… he started walking up the beach again, not wanting to lose sight of the blonde.

"Quinn, we need to talk alone for a moment." Oliver's hand was on Quinn's arm, pulling him to a stop. Quinn glanced at him and realized the guy's famously stoic British façade looked decidedly… uncomfortable.

A shiver of unease ran down Quinn's spine. "Oliver? What's wrong?"

He pulled back his hand, shoving both into the pockets of his pressed khaki shorts. "I'm not sure how to say this gently, so I won't try. Your mum called while the band was filming. Laura died last night."

"What?" Quinn's feet rooted in the sand. "But the last I heard she was better. She invited me stateside for Christmas."

Oliver shrugged, his expression overflowing with sympathy, handing a cell phone to Quinn. "You should call your mum back. The funeral is Saturday."

"But we... How would... Can I even..." Quinn wasn't sure what to say, let alone how to ask. The band was scheduled to stay through the weekend, play a few open air concerts so the director could add live concert footage to the video. But...

He had to go home. His cousin's wife had been like a big sister to him ever since high school, encouraging him to pursue his music. Four years older, she and his cousin Ed were the only ones in the family to support his decision to leave college a year early, when John and Grubber graduated. Laura was the one who'd smoothed things over with his parents.

Cancer, however, was an indiscriminate bitch.

As usual, Oliver was one step ahead. "There's a flight leaving the island tonight that'll get you to Jakarta. From there you're booked to L.A., and then a connector straight to Boston. It's more than twenty four hours of flying, but you'll make it in time."

Quinn nodded along. He trusted Oliver with the details. Except... "I'm not going through London? That's the faster way."

"Winter storms all across Europe. They've shut down Heathrow. The travel agent and I were at it for an hour and a half. You're circling the globe, and will have to sit around LAX for a few hours, but at least you'll get to Boston for the funeral."

A wave of a different emotion swept through Quinn, making his throat tight. Knowing that Oliver hadn't been able to wave his hand to fix this, but had taken the time to make sure Quinn would be okay... as both the youngest of three brothers and the youngest of eight cousins, it had been a long time since he'd felt like more than an afterthought.

Laura made him feel the same way too.

But now she was gone.

He swallowed hard, trying to push his emotions to the side and focus on logistics. "Ollie, I only brought beach clothes on this trip. I'll need a suit. Jeans. A coat. It's fucking freezing on Cape Cod in November."

"I'll give you a credit card. Charge whatever you need to the record company."

Another wave of emotion ripped through him. Quinn pulled the older man into a tight embrace. "Thank you. Seriously, the guys and I are so lucky to have you looking out for us."

"Just doing my job, Quinn."

"It's more than that and you know it. And we appreciate it."

After saying hasty goodbyes to his friends, and a very disappointed blonde in a teeny silver bikini, Quinn left the beach and hightailed it to the local airport. On the flight out of Jakarta, he overheard two of the flight attendants talking about harsh weather moving into the region over the next few days. Between his leaving and the rain headed toward the island, it was a good thing they'd finished shooting most of the music video. The additional concert footage would have to wait.

By the time Quinn landed in Boston, there were reports of a massive hurricane wreaking havoc along the coast of northern

Australia, moving toward Indonesia. The international reporters called it a "tropical cyclone" which was apparently what they called hurricanes in Australia. *Who knew?*

He texted Chuck and Grubber, saying he'd made it to Boston safe, and apologized again for leaving them. The replies came fairly quickly, considering the distance. *More girls for us,* Chuck texted back. Grubber's reply was longer. *The locals say they never have problems with hurricanes. Just an excuse to party harder. Don't worry about us.*

His thoughts so laser-focused on his own family tragedy, it hadn't occurred to Quinn to worry about the rest of the band. Hurricanes hit Cape Cod all the time. No big deal apart from a little wind damage. A few shingles off the roof, maybe a tree knocked down. Making it an excuse for heavy drinking sounded like an awesome idea, and he felt a twinge of jealousy. Here he was back in the U.S. for a funeral, and they were partying their asses off.

Directly in the path of Hurricane Nina.

Jake Campbell hates rules. Undercover to stop a drug ring at a posh Cape Cod resort, he can't resist the fiery head chef, Abbie Duncan. She may be on the suspect list, but he can't keep his hands to himself. With a rising body count, he must keep Abbie safe...but can he trust her with his jaded heart?

Excerpt from *Breaking the Rules*, published 2017 from Windmill Point Publishing:

Abigail Duncan planted both elbows on the bar and leaned in close, t-shirt pulling tight against her curves. After the day she'd had, this was one more headache she didn't want to deal with. "Level with me, Brian. How many has he had tonight?"

The bartender shook his head with a frown, looking her straight in the eye and ignoring her assets. "Like I said, Abbie, it's still his first pint. George has been nursing it for the last hour." He opened the cooler to grab several long necks, deftly flipping the caps as he plunked them onto a tray.

She heaved a sigh and let her shoulders relax a fraction. "Okay, I believe you. It's just that his doctor said he's not supposed to drink with his new meds."

"Yeah, but your dad can't watch the Red Sox with the guys and not have a beer in front of him." Brian gestured at the table of retired cops jeering at the big screen. "Stop being a spoilsport and let him have his fun."

Her shoulders stiffened again. "Honestly, I didn't know he'd be here when I decided to bring the Inn's kitchen crew for after-work drinks. There's only one sports bar in town, you know."

"It's all good. Try not to worry so much." Brian handed her the tray of drinks. "You sure you got this?"

She winked at him as she balanced the tray on her left hand, then made her way through the crowd of baseball fans.

Back at the foosball table in the corner, four of her co-workers engaged in a fierce battle. The rest crowded around to cheer them on. If today was any indication, her kitchen should run smoothly this summer. After all, Mothers' Day was one of the busiest days of the year – despite the $95 per person charge for the buffet spread. Everything went off without a hitch. Well, almost everything. It was a five-star restaurant. Something was always making the head chef apoplectic.

One of the new fry-cooks – *Dimitri? Or is that Matko? Those two are like peas in a pod* – scored a goal and raised both hands in victory while the other side began to protest. Raising her voice above the din, Abbie congratulated the winning team as she rested the tray of drinks on the edge of the foosball table. "This round's on me, you guys. Great job today." Eager hands reached for the long necks, clinking the bottles together in salute.

"To a great boss." Ian threw an arm around her shoulder to pull her close. He'd been the expediter in her kitchen for the past several summers, always choosing to winter somewhere warmer, whether Key West, Barbados, or this past year in L.A. "Your menu was genius, no matter what that fat bastard Delacorte says. If anything was a problem today, it was the big man's attitude."

Abbie felt her cheeks heat while everyone raised their bottles and voices in agreement. Francois Delacorte, the Executive Chef of Chatham's prestigious Atlantic Coastal Inn, wasn't one to mince words. There was no mistaking his outrage at discovering the kid-friendly choices discretely tucked away on a corner table at the Inn's exclusive buffet.

In Abbie's opinion, Delacorte's outrage was directly linked to his mile-wide misogynistic streak. Since his first day at the Inn, he'd taken an immediate dislike to both Abbie as Chef de Cuisine in the Inn's main dining room, and her coworker Miranda, the Executive Pastry Chef, and took every opportunity to belittle their abilities.

A hand jostled her shoulder. "Earth to Abbie," Ian said, laughter in his voice as she focused her gaze on him. "We lost you for a moment there." He clinked his bottle to hers. "Don't let him get to you."

She gave Ian a half smile and sipped her beer. She had to put up with the pompous Frenchman for a few more months before she had enough in her bank account. After years of taking orders from others, she was ready – *more than ready* – to strike out on her own. Her goal was to open her own restaurant before her thirtieth birthday, a mere year and a half away. One final summer at The Inn wouldn't kill her, but it certainly wouldn't be a cakewalk.

Tipping the bottle to her lips, Abbie drained the rest of her Bass Ale. Swiping the back of her hand across her mouth, she locked eyes with the most delicious hunk of blond stranger she'd seen in... well, in forever. He sat at one of the high top tables along the back wall, his wide shoulders and solid biceps stretching his shirt in intriguing ways. The smallest of smiles played across sculpted lips while he held her captive with his eyes. The air seemed to whoosh out of the room as she struggled to breathe under the intensity of his stare, each second lasting an eternity. She licked her suddenly dry lips, trying to grab the reins of her runaway libido.

The guy's dark-haired companion turned to follow his friend's gaze. The second man's lazy grin looked cocky as hell, raking his eyes up and down her body before giving her a deliberate nod and wink. *Really?* Abbie chuckled as she shook her head and turned away, the intensity of the moment evaporating like steam over a sauce pot. Ian nudged her with an elbow. "What's so funny?"

Abbie had more important things to focus on than some blond in a bar, no matter how godlike his physique. She smiled at her coworker. "Nothing. Nothing at all."

Jake Campbell frowned, his focus sliding away from the curvaceous redhead and back to his partner. "What do you think you're doing? Jeez, Garcia, we can't afford to screw up this job."

The other man snorted in disbelief. "Yeah, right. I saw you checking out her ass when she passed by with that tray of drinks."

Jake's voice lowered to an angry growl. "She works at the restaurant, you moron. Didn't you go through the case file?" Okay, so maybe he had been checking out her curves. A guy notices perfection when it walks by him.

"I don't remember any of those uptight cooks having an ass like that. This op gets better by the minute." Garcia tipped his beer bottle and leered toward the foosball table.

A surge of annoyance flared through Jake. "She's a suspect, not your personal eye candy. Her bank turned her down for a loan last year. Money problems are always a strong motivator. Plus, you're spending the next month working with her as your boss."

"Technically, the pastry cooks work for the Executive Pastry

Chef, who works in tangent with the Chef de Cuisine and reports directly to the Executive Chef."

"What the…?"

Garcia smiled. "My sisters both work in fancy Boston restaurants. I know the pecking order. Although working under that redhead sounds like it might be fun. Under her, on top of her… Hell, I can think of lots of interesting positions."

"Are you taking any of this seriously? We're chasing drug dealers, not one-night stands."

"I'm getting into my undercover persona. My character's a player, remember? Besides, one night with a woman who looks like that would never be enough."

"Garcia, take this seriously. We can't afford another op going south."

His friend's expression turned grim. "Dude, I'm acutely aware of our job responsibilities. You need to lighten up before you tank the rest of your career because of one stupid chick. You're thirty four, not dead."

Jake started to protest but Garcia held up one hand and shook his head. "Listen, Campbell, it's time you move on. I know Tessa broke your heart but she didn't chop off your dick."

Jake went still. "My ex has nothing to do with this."

"She has everything to do with your crappy attitude, and everything to do with you blowing your cover on a job we spent *three months* setting up. Three months of me sitting surveillance in that cockroach-infested apartment, all down the drain. Because of her."

Yeah, he couldn't deny that. Getting arrested for assault and making headlines while undercover was not Jake's most shining moment. "You should've put in for a new partner."

"When the captain offered us this undercover gig with Chatham P.D., I told you this was our chance to hit the restart button. Together. Get out from under that black cloud that's been dogging us. Plus, spring on Cape Cod is supposed to be awesome."

"As long as someone's happy," Jake grumbled. "I still think it's odd that the Chatham police chief reached out to Boston for undercover help. You'd think a town like this would be too small to hide a mole in the department."

"That's exactly the problem. In a town this small, everyone knows everyone, and it's probably second nature to put your friends above the law."

Jake grimaced. He may have crossed a few lines in the past, but how did any policeman justify breaking the law? Finishing the last of his beer, he pushed back his stool. "I need another drink."

"Because I brought up Tessa?" Garcia shook his head. "Let it go, man. Let *her* go."

"Believe me, I already have." Jake wasn't a forgive-and-forget kind of guy. He'd *never* forget the day he'd stopped by Tessa's apartment at lunchtime and found her skinny ass in bed with her yoga instructor. She claimed the sex meant nothing. That she loved Jake. *Yeah, right.* He didn't need Tessa's version of love.

"Want another beer or not?"

Garcia fished a twenty out of his wallet. "See what kind of tequila they've got back there too. I'm buying."

"Tequila?"

"Like Mama always says, it's not a celebration without tequila."

After two years as Garcia's partner, Jake was used to hearing what Mama had to say on practically every subject, but this was a new one. "What are we celebrating?"

Garcia smirked. "The fact that your junk didn't wither and

die. I saw the way you eyed the redhead. It's time you got on with your life."

Jake glanced over Garcia's head to where the woman in question pulled out her ponytail holder and ran her fingers through long, wavy locks that looked so soft, so touchable. She laughed at something her companion said, a throaty sound that twisted Jake's gut in a strange way.

Maybe Garcia was right. It was time to move on.